'You're no differe_____
serving drinks—y_____
Gate.'

Chance Mallory_____shock to the
gently-raised Eden Cortland. For the first time, she is
compelled by this rugged adventurer to confront the
bitter truth that her fortune comes from an infamous
gambling-saloon in San Francisco.

Rising to Chance's taunting challenge she throws in
her lot with the wild and reckless men and women of the
Barbary Coast. But can she overcome the barriers of
pride that stand between her and the forceful Chance
Mallory?

M. LOWES

From The
Flames

Robyn Stuart

MILLS & BOON LIMITED
London · Sydney · Toronto

First published in Great Britain 1983
by Mills & Boon Limited, 15–16 Brook's Mews,
London W1A 1DR

© Robyn Stuart 1983

Australian copyright 1983
Philippine copyright 1983

ISBN 0 263 74459 0

Set in 10 on 12 pt Linotron Times
04/1183–62,304

Photoset by Rowland Phototypesetting Ltd
Bury St Edmunds, Suffolk
Made and printed in Great Britain by
Cox & Wyman Ltd, Reading, Berks.

CHAPTER
ONE

EDEN had always known she'd had another life before coming to Miss Phelbert's.

A life in a house high on a hill, with a mother and a father and servants and a carriage and four. The trouble was she could remember so little of it.

She'd seen all the photographs of her home, with its grey towers and jutting chimneys and peaked roofs, of her mother, posed beneath a lacy white parasol, touring the Chicago World's Fair, partying with friends. Slender, dark eyed, pretty Victoria Cortland, always so proper.

There were far fewer pictures of her father. Very stiff in his silk top hat, his high-winged collar framing a strong featured face and deadened eyes, Tyler Cortland stared blankly out of the photograph album—frozen in anonymity for all eternity—as if he had deliberately sought to evade the camera's eye.

Yes, Eden had always known she'd had another life before coming to Miss Phelbert's. She had the pictures as proof. The trouble was she could find no sense of that life within herself. Except for the dream.

It was always the same, that dream. Just a shard of remembrance and no more. She would feel the fog curling across her face like a living thing. She would smell the scent of the sea, that briny, fresh bite of wind and water, carried by the fog up from the harbour.

The fog and the scent of the sea. Only those two things stood out against her mist-blurred memory of San Francisco, the city of her birth. Except for those bare fragments, Eden Cortland could catch no spark of that other life—could summon no sense of sadness when she thought of the yachting disaster that had taken both her parents.

After the accident, the house had been sold and Eden sent to Philadelphia. It was what her mother had always wanted. Nob Hill and its environs were all very satisfactory, but the rest of California was too boorish, too new for Victoria Cortland—and certainly for her daughter. Eden would go East to school, where the business of being a lady was taken very seriously. And even in death Victoria Cortland was not defeated.

At age seven, in accordance with her father's will and her mother's wishes, Eden came to Miss Phelbert's Academy for Young Women—and there she remained.

It was not an unpleasant place to grow up, this world of rigid etiquette and strict social sense. The students were given the finest of useless educations; trained to speak the Romance languages and play croquet with equal intensity, taught the intricacies of pouring tea, polite conversation, fine embroidery and—most importantly—how to cater to future husbands as dedicated to the life of privilege as they were themselves.

Like all the other girls Eden was an apt pupil. Diligently she practised the harp and piano, and spent long hours sitting with a riding crop stuck inside her belt to give her the straight back of the true lady.

Like all the other girls, she learned that the voice of a lady is well-modulated and even, that her head is held up and her eyes cast down. She learned that a lady took two milk baths a week and never went out in the sun without gloves and a hat. Like all the other girls she learned that a lady might play tennis, might bicycle, might even golf, but never with any enthusiasm, never without a corset —and certainly never well enough to best a man.

Under the careful tutelage of Harriet Phelbert and her hand-picked instructors, Eden learned to say the right words, learned to do the right things—learned to recognise the right people. Indeed, she scarcely knew any other kind existed.

The Saturday night soirées held for the older students were zealously chaperoned, only boys from totally acceptable families permitted. Holidays were spent with one or another of her school friends; riding to hounds in the Virginia tidewater—side-saddle of course— watching the polo matches on Long Island, taking the waters at Saratoga, doing the museums in Boston, mingling and conversing with men and women so alike as to have been shaped from the same mould.

Groomed to be sweet of face, docile of temperament, and above all ornamental, Eden was all of these, and yet sometimes, late at night, she would awaken from a dream-filled sleep possessed by a longing that would not be stilled. She would rush to the window, push open the sash and stare into the night, wondering—wondering what lay past the neat brick walls that seemingly forever had bounded her days, what lay beyond the manicured lawns and stone signpost that marked the Academy —and her life.

It was always the old dream that awakened her, the world thick with fog, heavy with the scent of the sea. And the longing, that was always the same too, unnamed, unknown, deep within her—a desire lost forever in the mist.

But in the morning the dream would be gone, the usual life would catch her back again. All would be as before—that is, until her eighteenth birthday.

'I've had a letter from San Francisco,' Miss Phelbert informed her that January morning, and quickly Eden masked her surprise.

There'd been a few letters over the past years from her guardian, always polite, always impersonal, but to be summoned to the Headmistress' office for the reading of one must mean something special.

Yet, hands folded decorously in her lap, Eden said only, 'Yes, Miss Phelbert?'

Harriet Phelbert nodded in approval. Overexcitement was a sign of poor breeding. Calmly she lifted the letter from her desk, unfastened her spectacles from the eyeglass button on her shirtwaist and pinched them on her nose.

'Now then. It seems that your guardian, Mr Cornelius Paxton, has passed on rather suddenly. But his son, Mr Julius Paxton, is only too happy to assume his responsibility. Now that you've reached your eighteenth birthday, he would like you to return to San Francisco, to the Paxton home. He and his mother wish to launch you into society there—and I quite agree with the idea.'

Once again Eden struggled to fight down her curiosity, this time with more difficulty, wringing her hands with such nervousness that Miss Phelbert paused, removed her spectacles and frowned. At this silent reproach, Eden drew a breath and was still.

Harriet Phelbert replaced her glasses.

'That's better. Naturally I've made enquiries into Mr

Paxton's character, his financial and social position, and I'm delighted to report that by all accounts he's as fine a gentleman as his father. He's sent a railroad ticket for you and a round trip ticket for a chaperon, first class compartment of course. I believe I shall send Miss Dill with you.'

Miss Phelbert paused again, this time to smile. 'I consider it a distinct point in Mr Paxton's favour that he does not possess one of those newfangled motor cars currenly being sold by Mr Henry Ford—a vulgar invention if ever I saw one.' She set down the letter, removed her spectacles and, taking a lace-trimmed, linen handkerchief from her shirtwaist pocket, began to wipe it industriously over the thick lenses.

'You've been with us a long time, Eden, I shall be saddened at your leaving—but proud as well. You've become a true lady while you have been with us—I can think of no higher compliment. It's time you took your rightful place in society.'

The whole school turned out to see Eden off. Demure, doe-eyed and all alike in their striped shirtwaists, dark tweed skirts and white serge box coats, the students of Miss Phelbert's Academy stood on the soot-blackened platform and waved a muted goodbye. But for all their training, they couldn't entirely wipe the excitement from their faces.

Only the day before Eden had been one of them. Now she stood grown up and elegant in a grey silk travelling suit banded with black velvet, grey kid gloves to her elbows. A fur capelet was about her shoulders, a dashing fur hat tipped low on her forehead, its twin feathers thrust bravely up against the elements, its gauzy veil covering her face to the chin. Every time she moved there was the discreet rustle of a taffeta petticoat, and looped over one wrist was a totally wonderful, totally useless fur muff.

And the very thought of where she was going! When their turns came they would scatter no farther than Boston or Baltimore, Virginia or Long Island. Eden alone would be crossing a continent. And Miss Phelbert had told them that while it was winter in Philadelphia, there would be roses growing in San Francisco—the grass as green as spring!

Seating herself in her compartment, the very picture of fashionable womanhood. Eden waved sedately in her turn. But her eyes, flashing beneath the veil, were alive, alert. Inside she was quivering with excitement.

But what for? A city she could not recall? People she could not remember?

There was a piercing whistle, a rain of cinders, a jerk forward, backward, and forward once more, and the train began moving. Face pressed to the window, Eden watched the city of Philadelphia fade into snow-swept fields, but in her mind's eye it was the Academy—her life—she was seeing slip away.

With each grinding, clacking turn of the wheels, the miles between her past and her future were lengthening.

But to where, to what was she heading?

For as long as she could remember her life had been orchestrated by Miss Phelbert, each day following the one before in its sameness, each day secure with the knowledge of what the next one would bring.

But now—?

*   *   *

The train trip to California took seven days—Miss Dill snoring most of them away in blissful ignorance. As the chaperon had told Eden at the onset of the journey, 'If I'm forced to leave Philadelphia to travel half-way across the country on a smoke-snorting monster, I shall endeavour to do so as painlessly as possible!'

And so she did. Only for meals did Agnes Dill's small, birdlike body twitch to consciousness—and these, of course, she ordered sent in. If ever she did leave their compartment, it was with her eyes straight ahead and a scented handkerchief pressed firmly to her nose.

'Undesirables,' she would mutter as soon as she and Eden were ensconced in comfortable solitude. 'This train is filled with undesirables!' Then underscoring her statement with a furious jab of her hatpin, she would set back her veil and promptly fall asleep once again.

Yet in Miss Dill's determined slumber Eden found a freedom greater than she'd ever imagined. Nervously at first, gloved hands clenched hard before her, then with growing bravery—mounting curiosity—she explored the world beyond her compartment. A world beyond her ken.

A world of apple-cheeked immigrant women and their moustachioed husbands. A world of gaunt midwestern farmers and their stocky sunburnt women. A world populated with people who wore their red bandannas and their callouses with pride, who ate onions and sausage with lip-smacking gusto. A world rampant with noise and colour and the headlong spirits of those eager to begin a new life.

Like Eden's own spirits the day she'd boarded the train to San Francisco, like all her awakenings from those fog-filled nights. Watching these people, listening to them—while always distant, always shy—Eden yet knew a bond with them.

Her excitement for the city of her birth—and her dreams—began to mount.

In the foment of an orange-coloured dawn, the train pulled into the Oakland mole and Eden and Miss Dill boarded the ferry for the trip across the bay. Heedless of her chaperon's warning that fresh air had an adverse effect on a lady's complexion, it was from the wind-whipped deck that Eden watched the panorama of San Francisco rise before her eyes.

Sweeping right, sweeping left, were hills—always and everywhere hills! In all directions the city rose and fell, as if filled with such zest it could lie level for only a block or two at a time.

To one side was the cliff that Eden recognised from Miss Phelbert's description—Telegraph Hill, its seaward side rising a sheer 150 feet. On its slopes dwelt the Mexicans, their low houses bounded with balconies, and the Italians too were there, their cottages tumbling crazily one atop the other.

Beyond this precipice was Russian Hill—the highest point in a city of heights.

From this apex, Eden let her eyes drop to the bay —fifty miles of water spread out like a sheet of gold, forested with masts. Across this yellow flood waited the wharves, and as the ferry pulled closer, Eden leaned forward in eagerness, gripping the salt-sticky rail with both hands. For on San Francisco's waterfront met the ways of the world.

Here turbanned Hindus walked beside brown-skinned Samoans and black-skinned Africans. Here Neapolitans sailed their fishing boats through misty dawns. Here whalers raised crews and adventurers sought money to wrest treasure ships from the ocean's depths.

Here—below and above them—was the new life those people on the train had hoped for—journeyed so far for. Here in the pulsing city of San Francisco waited the answer to their quest.

And Eden Cortland's quest?

Like the echo of a life she had almost forgotten, Eden suddenly saw the Paxton carriage. The morning sunshine bouncing off its glass windows, its crest shining gold, it rose up in subdued elegance beside the white ferry building.

Miss Dill was overjoyed to step again into the world of privilege and she sank back against the padded brocade seats with a sigh of contentment. But as the carriage edged through boxes and barrels and roistering sailors, Eden kept her eyes on the waterfront. As if gathering memories—mementoes—she could not look away.

Their destination was Nob Hill, where the powerful clustered like gods on Mount Olympus. Here the true nabobs of the city lived, men who had made their money on silver and gold—and corruption, some said. High above the scraping mass of humanity they lived, secure within their citadels of marble and granite—and wealth.

And here, grander than all the other hilltop palaces, was Paxton Place.

It was a vast house of grey stone fronted by marble columns, its terraced gardens sweeping grandly away on all sides. As if to mark its awesome splendour for all time, four turreted towers rose stark against the sky.

Beyond the wrought-iron fence, high marble steps swept up to the massive brass door, and beside this door

stood a servant, stiffly waiting. Waiting to usher Eden
Cortland from dream to reality.

Waiting to lead her from what might have been to
what must always be.

From her seat at the head table, Eden cast a look across
the banqueting room to where long double windows
opened on to the garden. Seen through the mesh of the
lace curtains, the fog hung over the night like a veil.

Eden shut her eyes, longing for the cooling dampness
of that fog against her face, wishing for the stirring of the
wind against her skin, the scent of the sea in her nostrils.

The fog and the scent of the sea . . . Would whatever
portent they held for her be forever out of reach?

'You're a triumph tonight, my dear!'

Eden started at the sound of the silken voice. Nervously she clenched one hand hard against the damask
tablecloth.

'Thank you . . . Julius.' Even after a week the name
did not come easily.

Julius Paxton smiled, the corners of his mouth drawing back to a careful line that disturbed no part of the
perfect oval of his face. Indeed, from head to foot, he
was a picture of perfect symmetry, his cutaway coat
hanging in folds as smooth as his skin, his thinning hair
growing back in two precise points from either temple.
As he leaned closer the faint, fine odour of sandalwood
seemed to seep from the pores of his small, slim body.

'Just look about you, Eden—the cream of San Francisco society is at your feet tonight!'

Obediently Eden followed the sweep of her guardian's gaze up and down the long tables that criss-
crossed the room, each one flanked by shimmering

women in silken gowns and sleek men in starched white shirt fronts.

Each one was an oasis of muted conversation, the tempered chatter rising and falling as the courses were served and sampled. Clear consommé in a cut glass tureen, cracked crab nestled in a bed of sculpted ice, boiled salmon, Cheshire cheese, golden brandy in crystal goblets.

And as a fitting frame for this feast, these men and women, was the banqueting hall itself—the panelled walls polished to a high sheen, the floors covered with Persian rugs. From behind the bevelled glass doors of a mahogany buffet glittered an array of Oriental antiquities, beside it stood a Japanese silk screen, softly painted with dragons and waterfalls and almond-eyed maidens. Even the newly-installed electric lights had been well dimmed, hidden behind china shades.

The people, the room—even the subtle music of the string quartet playing in one corner—all formed the warp and weave of the finest of tapestries, aloof, elegant, and oh, so correct.

And part of this tapestry, Eden knew, was she herself, poised and painted by Julius Paxton. Her ivory satin gown had been his selection, the diamonds that sparked a colourless fire about her throat and banded her hair, his gift.

'You've been a caged bird far too long, Eden my dear,' Julius went on in that silvered voice. 'But tonight you've begun to break through the bars.'

So saying, he moved his hand to cover hers—and at his touch Eden flinched.

She did not know why. Perhaps it was the feel of that hand, featherlight, with a spidery strength. Perhaps it was the look of the manicured nails, slightly blue tinged, as if his body gave off no heat.

Or was it the dim light reflecting off his spectacles —waving the glass like water and hiding his eyes?

Julius did not seem to notice her hesitation. His smile stayed intact. Her hand stayed imprisoned.

Without warning the balcony doors banged open. The music stopped. Swansdown fans stilled. Forks were halted mid-way to open mouths. Every head snapped swiftly around to see, framed against the fog, a man.

He was tall, wide in the shoulder, slim in the hip, and in cuffed trousers his legs were slightly apart. There was an animal wariness to the angled set of his head, a hawkish thrust to his hard features, to the thin, high-bridged nose and clefted, jutting chin. A seam ran the length of either cheek, grooves marking the corners of his eyes, the rugged lines of his face hiding his precise age—he might have been thirty or a few years younger.

Dark auburn hair grew thick and long across his forehead and fell over the collar of his carelessly unbuttoned jacket, the open neck of his rough linen shirt showing a thatch of burnished hair at the base of his throat.

For the space of a heartbeat—for the span of a breath—the man said nothing, nor did he move. And like a tangible thing Eden felt the sinewy strength of his long, hard-muscled body reach across the room to hold them all motionless.

Then deliberately he turned his head and looked at Eden.

Her heart lurched. Hot blood stained her cheeks. Never in her life had she been looked at as this stranger was looking at her, his gaze totally devoid of deference —respect.

With a contempt that struck like a blow, he ran his glance from the lush, blue-black coils of her hair to the creamy whiteness of her throat and shoulders, over the small, proud upflare of her breasts, down the silken lines of her body. Then once more he returned his eyes to her face and as he did, a gust of wind shot through the open windows and spiralled across the room. Despite the heat of her body, Eden shivered.

Now the stranger came forward, moving between the tables with a definite tread—his powerful body seeming to possess the very ground it walked on. The shocked murmurs of the glittering men and women swept after him, all eyes turning to their host.

Yet Julius was silent, staring, one hand still holding Eden's.

The stranger stopped before the head table. With a studied coolness he pulled a fistful of dollars from his pocket and threw them down before Julius Paxton.

'The poke due on the Silver Dollar, Mr Paxton.'

Julius' silken voice was suddenly sharp.

'You've chosen an odd time for business, sir. But perhaps I can mark it down to your obvious lack of breeding.' He brushed the money aside. Then, as if he had touched something unclean, he lifted his damask napkin and carefully wiped his hands.

The gesture was not lost on the stranger. Slowly he smiled, his firm lips stretching into a tight line to show animal white teeth. 'If it's you Nob Hill gents that have all the manners,' he said in a voice that was heavy and deep and too controlled, 'why don't you introduce me to Miss Cortland?'

A ripple ran through the crowd—and in a small, uneven rush Eden let out her own breath, unaware she had been holding it. Softly, dazedly, she stammered, 'You know my name—'

'I know more than that.'

He leaned forward, setting heavy hands on the table, and Eden saw that his eyes were blue, hard as steel, and in their depths was a hatred that brought forth a sudden sweep of memory.

She had seen those eyes, that hatred before.

Or had she?

'Do I—do I know you?'

'Do you?' Except for a biting edge the stranger's question betrayed no emotion. 'Do you?'

A moment more that hatred blazed, and then a veil dropped over his gaze. Eden's memory—if it had been there at all—vanished.

'Eden, go to your room! I will not have you a party to this!'

Bred to obedience, Eden Cortland swept quickly to her feet. Her voice was muted. 'Yes, Julius.'

But as she turned to go, the stranger caught her glance once more. As if baiting her—as if seeing how hard, how far he could push her—his eyes challenged her.

'Eden!' There was frozen anger on Julius' face, the distended nostrils cutting deep lines into the smooth skin. 'I said go to your room.'

Eden turned.

'Are you afraid to meet me, Miss Cortland?'

The voice was cool, as cool as the steely gaze Eden felt piercing her back. Everything she'd been taught, every-thing she'd ever known told her to leave the room—to obey. Yet abruptly she came about. From some unknown place deep inside, fierce words bubbled up.

'I'm afraid of nothing—and no one!'

Something flickered behind the stranger's eyes and was gone. He grinned. 'Then let me introduce myself. I'm—'

'Please!' Julius' interruption rang with vicious politeness. 'You must permit me to do the honours! And since you're so determined to be privy to this Eden, I shall spare you nothing.'

Julius stretched out a black-clad arm towards the stranger, and looking from one man to the other, Eden was conscious of a current pulsing between the two—a tension that went beyond this place, this time.

'This is Chance Mallory—born and bred on the Barbary Coast. His world is three solid blocks of gambling dens and saloons and squalor. His intimates, the very dregs of society!'

Julius moved a precise step backwards, his hand going to the servants' bellpull that hung overhead. 'But you've overstepped yourself tonight, Mallory, venturing out of your sewer without protection. Once my men get hold of you—'

Julius' words were interrupted by a shudder that seemed to shake the house to its very foundation. The walls trembled. The floorboards quivered. The room tilted crazily, sending plates and goblets smashing to the floor, throwing Eden backwards, her shoulders hitting hard against the wall.

The electric lights flickered once and went out. In the blackness Eden heard every sound as if magnified— Julius' clipped commands to the servants, the crescendo of frantic screams, a single frenzied wail, repeated over and over, 'Earthquake! Earthquake!'

Quite near, Eden heard Chance Mallory's contemptuous mutter, 'Passel of fools, it was only a second's tremor.'

Senses sharpened by fear, Eden knew Mallory was moving nearer—and nearer still, so close she could feel his presence beside her like some watching, waiting cat.

Deliberately she arched her body away from the wall and took a step, but even as she moved, he was beside her. Instinctively she flung out an arm, as if to ward him off, but he seized her hand and spun her against him with a force that drove the breath from her lungs.

He clamped a hand over her mouth, his voice welling up in a low, humourless laugh, and she could feel his breath hot on her neck.

'Sometimes a tremor can be damned convenient.'

Her back to his chest, his forearm hard across her breasts, Chance Mallory, half dragged, half carried her through the darkness and to the open window. As they emerged into the night she felt him draw a quick breath, relaxing his powerful body for just an instant—and in that instant Eden kicked out at him, twisting her mouth against his hand so that her teeth cut into his skin.

He cursed violently, and as his grip came away, Eden plunged forward—only to be yanked brutally back, her scream stifled with a gag.

'Witch!' With one swing of his arm, Mallory hefted her over his shoulder. 'I didn't think you had that much fight in you. Well, hang on, you're going for a little ride.'

He began to descend the garden steps, Eden bouncing against him like a sack of meal. The night was still and wet and choked with fog. The distracted voices in the barking of a dog all echoed muffled and distant, and as if from another world.

This world held only the reality of Chance Mallory and her own terror, so palpable a thing it was a burning knot in her lungs.

Too sharply he swung around a corner, Eden's head striking one of the ornamental pillars that marked the garden fence. A blazing light flashed before her eyes, as if to slice away forever all the mists of her past.

And then she was swallowed whole by the fog.

CHAPTER
TWO

RAUCOUS ragtime music began beating at the edge of Eden's brain—bringing her back to dim awareness. She blinked twice, trying to dispel the strange haze that hung before her eyes, trying to discover the source of that strange music.

Trying to discover where she was.

Groggily she ran her gaze around the unfamiliar room, seeing a straight-backed chair—a small wooden table.

Seeing Chance Mallory.

Now her memory came back with a rush. At once she tried to rise, but a searing pain in her temple drove her down again—and she realised with a start that she was lying on a bed.

Chance Mallory's bed? Her eyes went wide in horror.

As if he had read her thoughts, Mallory grinned like a malicious tomcat. 'That's right, it's my room—I work downstairs. I carried you up the back way. In case you're interested, you made the trip from Nob Hill in a hell cart.' His hard lips gave a sudden, sardonic twist. 'Too bad you weren't awake—I'm sure you would have enjoyed the ride.'

He came forward, and there was about him a sense of leashed tension straining beneath the mockery—a cold glitter to his eyes fiercer than anger. He held out a glass.

'How about a toast to your first night on the Barbary Coast, Miss Cortland?'

But the contents of the glass looked suspiciously like liquor. Eden managed a bare shake of her head. 'I—I don't drink spirits—'

Mallory dropped to one knee beside the bed and pressed the glass to her mouth, forcing the liquid between her lips. 'I said drink it.'

The whiskey seared her tongue and scorched her throat, bringing the tears to her eyes. But as she drew a gasping breath, Mallory poured down another mouthful and another. He stood.

'That ought to help some. I'm sorry about the bruise you took—that wasn't in the plan.'

For a moment more the liquor's fire burnt with a raw flame, gradually melting down to but a pleasant warmth that flowed into every part of Eden's body, blurring the throbbing pain at her temple. She lay very still, letting the whiskey's glow steal over her, and watched Chance Mallory.

He walked first to the table to set down the glass, then came to the window, his stride light yet powerful, every footfall firmly placed. Deliberately he set both hands against the sill—hands too hardened for gentility, the burnished hair lying thick against his powerful wrists, the tendons standing out like ropes.

Eden had never seen a man's hands like those. She'd never seen a room like this one.

The wooden floors were bare, the walls empty of ornamentation, a single naked bulb was suspended on a rough cord from the ceiling. Like the man who occupied it, this room revealed nothing, asked nothing.

Without turning, Mallory spoke, drawling out his

words in a gibing kind of wonder. 'I never thought I'd
have Eden Cortland resting so easily in my bed.'

Eden froze. In sharp humiliation she stared at the
broad back.

What had she been thinking of, to behave in this way?
Relaxing indolently on a man's bed—and not a gentleman's bed to be sure! Thick, heavy shame, fierce as
the whiskey, surged through her veins. As if she were
struggling for air, her breath began to come in choking
jerks.

Then abruptly she stood and lifted her head. Her
shame fell away, replaced by an unaccustomed spirit.
How dared a man like Chance Mallory think he could
insult her so! Well, he would not have the last word.

'You have no right to speak to me in such a way, Mr
Mallory!' Her voice, vibrant and deep flowing, sounded
strange to her ears—as unfamiliar as her anger—but she
felt a surge of pride at her own mettle, at the brave words
welling up, as they had earlier, from some unknown
place inside. 'I don't know why you've brought me here,
but I demand that you take me back to Paxton Place at
once!'

Mallory's shoulders stiffened and he swung slowly
around, assuming the stance he'd had when he'd in-
vaded the party, feet spread wide, head at an angle.

But Eden held her ground before him—and the determination with which she squared her shoulders and
raised her chin was nothing she had been taught, but
something inbred and instinctive and all her own.

Her face had been wiped clean of docility, the strong
sweep of her cheek showed plainly, her generous mouth
no longer curved to sweetness but stretched to its natural
contours, full and firm. Against the ivory pallor of her

skin her black, slanted brows and tip-tilted eyes cut a startlingly resolute line, the inky black lashes swept up to show unwonted fire in her dark gaze as she stared up at Chance Mallory.

'Don't look at me like I'm your lackey!'

Mallory exploded across the room and seized her arms above the elbow. As if it had never been, Eden's new-found strength crumpled in his grip.

His hawklike profile, hewn as if from granite, loomed over her. Her head barely reached to his shoulder.

'You're in no position right now to tell me anything, Miss Cortland.' His steely eyes drove deep into her own, forcing home the threat in his words. Just remember that.'

With an abruptness that sent her staggering against the iron bedstand, Chance released her and the bruising marks of his fingers showed red on her flesh. He poured out a drink, twisting the glass in one hand as he looked at her, and a muscle worked fiercely in his heavy jaw.

'I brought you here because I thought it was time you saw something—found out something—and when you do, by God, you won't be so high and mighty.'

He downed the drink, then set the glass against the table with a thump and strode past her to the door, flinging it open. The discordant blare of music and laughter filled the room and, taut lips curling into a sneer, Mallory nodded back at her.

'After you, Miss Cortland.'

Somehow Eden pushed herself erect. She ran trembling hands over her hair, over her skirt, and came forward into the hall, where a narrow staircase circled up two flights from below.

Somehow she started down those stairs, somehow her

head was poised correctly, somehow her steps were
measured and precise. But the ruse was a pitiful one. She
was sick with fear, of this man—this place.

They emerged on to a landing. A wide, red-carpeted
stairway stretched out before them, leading the way to
an enormous room below—a room where long windows
were framed with gold tasselled draperies and the walls
were papered with red velvet. A room where the dazzle
of the circular chandeliers was given back again and
again in the gilt-framed mirrors and long pier-glasses.

A row of fluted pillars stretched from frescoed ceiling
to floor, dividing the gilded room in half. To the left of
the columns was a stage hung with gold velvet curtains
and fronted by a row of winking footlights. While piano,
banjo, fiddle, trumpet and trombone wailed out the
Maple Leaf Rag from the orchestra pit, a line of over-
rouged and underdressed young women, arms linked,
hoofed and kicked across the stage in exuberant—if
relative—time to the music. Their gaudy costumes were
cut low enough to reveal an ample amount of flesh and
short enough to display dimpled knees and rounded
calves encased in black net stockings.

Circling the stage were small tables at which clusters
of dandified young men sat on red velvet chairs enjoying
the show and ogling the satin-spangled barmaids. Now
and then they did more than ogle, grabbing at the girls
for a well-aimed pinch on a well-rounded bottom. The
girls responded in turn, some with a kiss, some—to the
ribald laughter of the men—with an equally well-placed
right to the jaw.

To the right of the pillars was devoted exclusively to
serious drinking and gambling. In white shirts and black
waistcoats, sporting red garters on their white sleeves,

ten bartenders stood at the ready behind the polished curve of the mahogany bar. There were no fewer than eight green baize gaming tables, a life-size portrait of a nubile and naked young woman over each one, before which all manner of men were packed six or seven deep, dudes decked out in canary-coloured suits and diamond shirt studs, walrus-moustached gentlemen sporting spats and canes, thickset Russian sailors in black sweaters, Italian fishermen in gaudy shirts and sashes.

A smokey, bluish haze hung just below the ceiling, and the air was thick with the smell of tobacco and liquor, spiced with the cheap scent of the women's perfume and the dandy's hair pomade. Voices blended into a single, sibilant buzz, the hum broken occasionally by a shrill female laugh or a winner's lusty shriek. But the snap of the cards, the click of the ivory balls in the roulette wheel, the rattle of the faro box, these sounds pierced through the music and laughter.

And, louder than anything else, came the dealer's strident cries,

'Five hundred dollar limit, gentlemen, five hundred!'

'All bets in, gentlemen!'

'Keep your eye on the turn of the card!'

'And the wheel spins, gentlemen, will it be red or black?'

'Jack wins! Jack wins!'

Grabbing at the railing, Eden stared into the world below, a world she'd never even known existed, a mad kaleidoscope of blinding glitter and garish music, of clinking glasses and rolling dice, of jostling, shouting, roistering, half-clad women and reckless men.

'The Golden Gate,' Chance Mallory said in a strangely intense tone. 'What do you think of it?'

Eden looked at him and her head lifted on the arched, slender throat. 'I think it's vile. Now may I go?'

'So, you think it's vile do you?'

Mallory braced his back against the railing and folded his heavy arms across his chest. Yet there was something guarded in the lazy pose, as if his every muscle was tensed. Like a cat toying with a mouse, he watched her—and Eden realised he was relishing her discomfort.

'It's too bad you feel that way, Miss Cortland—considering the Golden Gate has paid your bills all these years.'

Eden stared at him, uncomprehending. 'What do you mean?'

'I mean your father owned the Golden Gate—or at least the largest part. It's the profits from this place that kept your family on Nob Hill—that kept you riding high out East.'

Like someone just stunned by a blow, Eden's lips went white; her face as still as death. She moved from the railing into the hallway, her steps dazed, her brain struggling to take in what he'd said—even as she refuted it. Slowly she shook her head.

'You must be mad! My father would never have been associated with a place like this—a cheap, common saloon—'

'Get it straight, Miss Cortland,' Mallory's voice cracked like a whip, 'it's this cheap saloon that's kept you living like a lady! You're no different from any of those girls on the stage or serving drinks—you both make your living off the Golden Gate!'

With all the strength she possessed, Eden drew back her arm and slapped Chance Mallory across the face. 'How dare you say such things to me!'

Mallory held motionless. There was a rigid set to his mouth and in his blue eyes Eden saw again that hard, simmering hatred. She could hear his heavy breathing, hear her own heart beating furiously.

'You little coward,' he ground out between clenched teeth. 'I thought you said you weren't afraid of anything. Well, why don't you admit it—you're afraid to face the truth.'

The long wail of a single trumpet blasted the air —pierced the moment—slicing through the current of tension that bound them.

A soundless cry clutching at her throat, Eden tore free—of Chance Mallory's eyes, his words. She pushed past him, stumbling to the stairs.

It was the pit of hell that was waiting below, she knew that now, waiting to devour her. But it was her only way out and she must take it. Gathering up her skirts, she ran down the stairs and plunged into the throng.

Heedless of the catcalls that followed her flight, the coarse laughter, she pushed against the crowd. Once, she felt rough hands at her waist, but she twisted violently free. As she neared the swinging doors they were flung wide by a covey of reeling sailors. Straight as an arrow she shot through their midst and on to the street. And there she stopped.

In both directions the street was ablaze with light, awash with music and laughter, teeming with shouting, brawling men and beckoning harlots. Pedestrians dodged carriages, carriages dodged motor cars, the dusty roads were churned to soft, thick mud by the constant flow of traffic.

More crowded than Philadelphia's main thoroughfare on a Sunday afternoon, it was far, far noiser, pulsing with a kind of rough, vital life the sedate streets of the East never saw.

Caught within the Golden Gate, Eden had thought only of escape, But now she knew there was no way out and no way back. From the Barbary Coast to Paxton Place stretched a distance as long as eternity.

'Lookin' fer somethin', or someone, little lady?'

From a nearby building, a man weaved towards Eden, bottle in one hand. Quickly she moved backwards. A new fear grabbed at her. But her shaking steps brought her hard against Chance Mallory, the swinging doors of the Golden Gate flung wide behind him.

'The lady's just leaving.'

The pointed words, backed up by the powerful physique, sent the drunken stranger staggering in another direction.

Why Chance Mallory had helped her, Eden didn't know. But then she knew nothing of him—or his world.

Hesitantly she looked up at him. 'Thank you,' she murmured softly, and to her own ears her voice sounded strange and far away.

'Don't waste your finishing school manners on me,' Mallory answered her harshly, heavy jaw hard. He stepped past her and on to the street, and lifting one hand, commanded a hackney cab to pull close. He tossed a coin up to the driver. 'Paxton Place.'

Without ceremony Mallory turned back and swung Eden off her feet, lifting her over the mud to deposit her carelessly on the padded leather seat. 'Get back to Nob Hill and stay there. You're not woman enough for the Barbary Coast.'

CHAPTER
THREE

It couldn't be true. It couldn't be true.

Over and over the words ground through Eden's mind. It couldn't be true.

They were the pounding rhythm of the carriage wheels, those words, a constant drumbeat against her brain. It couldn't be true. Tyler Cortland couldn't have been associated with such a place—such people. It couldn't be true.

Or could it?

Julius was waiting in the library when she returned to Paxton Place. The electricity had not yet been restored and a single silver candelabra lit the room, throwing an uncertain light against the shelves and shelves of leather-bound books, silhouetting Julius Paxton's small, slim frame as he stood with his back to her.

He pivoted but slightly as she entered, revealing the stem of a brandy snifter lightly supported in his right hand. From the folds of his satin dressing-gown rose the odour of sandalwood.

'Eden, my dear! How wonderful to have you home safely! You're well—unharmed?'

Hesitating in the doorway, pale and dishevelled, the bruise darkening against her temple, Eden felt a near paralysing weakness in every bone and muscle. Yet she knew she must hold out a little longer—there would be answers required, explanations.

'I'm quite well, Julius,' she said evenly.

'Excellent! Excellent!'

A small, circular motion of Julius' wrist sent the golden liquid swirling against the sides of the glass. 'Immediately on realising your absence, I sent a fleet of my men to comb the city. They soon reported to me where you were—and whom you were with.'

He paused and passed the snifter consideringly beneath his nose.

'Had the rogue kept you confined for any length of time, I would have taken—steps—to handle the matter, but since you're safe—well—' Julius took a measured sip of brandy. 'It's best to let the situation rest now. Unfortunately Chance Mallory will probably never see justice for this escapade. The authorities are powerless on the Barbary Coast.'

Almost imperceptibly, Julius' hand tightened against the goblet, his silken voice growing but a fraction more clipped, the rounded tones becoming more precise. Yet that very smoothness held an odd intensity.

'The Barbary Coast is a disgrace to all of San Francisco—it should be eliminated!'

Abruptly—the abruptness startling in one so suave —Julius drained his glass. He streaked out one hand to tug on the servants' bellpull. Then slowly he turned, his lips drawn back into that small, careful smile.

'I did not like your rebellious behaviour at dinner tonight, Eden. I find this tendency to disobedience most distressing in one of your breeding, your blood—in a lady of your quality. I hope I will not notice it again.'

With a sharp little gesture Eden brought her hands against the front of her skirt. 'I'm sorry, Julius. I didn't mean to distress you. You've been most kind to me.'

'We won't speak of it again. I suggest a good night's sleep as the best remedy for this unfortunate evening. Ah—Chang!'

Surprised, Eden glanced to the doorway to see a servant standing there. She had not heard anyone approach. The Oriental wore puffed blue pantaloons, the sleeves of his brocade tunic falling long over his wrists, and in his right hand he held a branched candel-abra high. His lemon-coloured face was broad and bland and of indeterminate age and his black eyes shone like opaque jet. Flat against his skull was a small, round, black cap.

'Chang will light you to your room, Eden.'

Julius dipped his head towards the door and silently the servant bowed his head in return. He pivoted and on slippered feet made his way once again into the hall, black *queue* swinging against his back. With practised grace, Eden made a small curtsey and followed him, but mid-step, Julius halted her.

'Eden—'

The corners of Julius Paxton's careful smile seemed to harden—the fine odour of sandalwood seeming to thick-en in the air about them, the gloom seeming to gather around them.

As Eden had discerned a strange intensity behind that silken voice, so now was she conscious of something hidden behind the silken manner. Something hidden behind the moment. An odd, unnamed premonition began bubbling in her breast.

'Eden,' he said again, 'Chance Mallory—did he speak to you of anything disturbing?'

Eden sucked in a rapid breath. Deliberately she dou-bled her hands into hard fists, as if to squeeze forever from her memory the power of a steely gaze, the sting of violent words. As if to hide from Julius Paxton the burning question gnawing at her.

Her voice was steady, almost automatic, as she answered him. 'Chance Mallory said—nothing.'

Julius gave a brief nod of acknowledgement—of dismissal. Once more he turned away, leaving Eden staring at his satin-clad back. There had been no ripple across that perfect face, his eyes—hidden behind the thick lenses—had revealed nothing. Yet Eden sensed, as the bubble of suspicion built in her breast, that Julius Paxton knew she was lying—and more.

It couldn't be true. It couldn't be true. To the rhythm of those words Eden climbed the stairs behind the silent Chang, following his soundless path to her bedroom.

It couldn't be true. It couldn't be true. Like a black snake the words slithered in and out of her every breath as the maid readied her for sleep.

But sleep would not come.

It couldn't be true. It couldn't be true. All during the long night those words bit at her brain. They greeted her before dawn, forcing her up from the enormous four-poster bed, beating at her until, finally, she slumped before the dressing-table and, head buried in her arms, mumbled aloud, 'Could it be true?'

'Victoria Cortland's daughter.'

Like the rustle of dry leaves a thin voice whispered into the room. Unsure that she had even heard it, thinking perhaps she was dreaming, Eden lifted her head. Pushing back the tumbled hair from her eyes, she saw reflected in the dressing-table mirror a woman standing close behind her.

She was small and frail and wore a trailing négligé of

dark silk, her grey hair streaming unbound over her shoulders. There was a faded prettiness about the fine bones of her face and in her deep-set eyes, a faraway look.

The woman lifted hands as thin and white as blue veined marble and began to run them restlessly over Eden's hair, her shoulders, all the while staring intently into the oval glass. Her own reflection was vacant—so vague as to appear disembodied, while Eden's face, framed by the mass of black hair, was tinged with fear, her bewildered eyes searching the empty ones behind her.

'You have your mother's hair, so very long and thick —and her skin, so white! But you're not so pretty as Victoria, you have more of your father's look to your face.'

The woman sighed and straightened and began an idle path about the room, hands picking nervously at the silken sleeves of her nightgown. She walked with grace but without aim, as if her physical presence and her spirit were separate things, her body moving from long habit, her mind never quite at ease.

'I knew you were awake—I heard you tossing and turning all last night . . . I didn't think you'd mind if I came to visit you. I'm Lenore Paxton, Julius' mother. I'm sorry for not meeting you sooner—for not attending the festivities last night—but I've been unwell . . .' She passed a vague hand over her forehead. 'I've been ill so much lately . . .'

Quickly Eden stood. Belting her wrapper about her waist, she came to Lenore's side and took her arm, and gratefully the woman sagged against her, her weight a negligible thing. Gently Eden led her to the velvet *chaise.* 'Please, lie down. Shall I ring for someone?'

'No—no . . .'

Head back, eyes closed, Lenore Paxton's face bore the fleshless look of a skull, the skin stretched tightly over the delicate bones. She began moving her hands in a little circular motion against her forehead.

'Soon Chang will come with my medicine—and then I'll sleep . . . It will be such a peaceful sleep, filled with memories . . . pleasant memories . . .' A smile grazed her lips. 'Your parents will be in those memories. Pretty, pretty Victoria, with so many fine plans and dreams —and Tyler—and even you, my dear, as a young child . . .'

Eden dropped to her knees beside the *chaise.* Her hands were clasped in her lap and her black eyes were blazing, there was a tautness to every slender line of her body, to every bone and muscle. Her heart was pounding out a dull ache at the back of her head—the beats filling her throat so that polite hedging was impossible. She could manage only forthrightness now.

'You knew my parents well—you must tell me something! Is it true—did my father own the Golden Gate saloon?'

Slowly Lenore's heavy lids lifted. 'How do you come to ask me that, child?'

Eden made a frantic dismissing motion with her clasped hands. 'How I found out is not important. Is it true?'

'It is.'

As if she'd fallen on a sharp stick, Eden felt a physical pain tearing at her breast. She pressed her hands across her bodice as if to a wound. 'But how—' She could not go on.

But Lenore needed no prompting. She had slipped away to a world of her own, a world of shadows, and was speaking freely.

'Victoria never knew of course, it would have killed her—killed her place in society—and that was always the most important thing to Victoria Cortland. No one ever knew—except my husband, he was the executor of the estate. And Julius . . . I discovered it only by accident—one day I saw some papers I shouldn't have. Julius was so angry when he found out I knew—'

Abruptly Lenore stopped. She stood and began once more to wander the room, her deep-set eyes distracted, her hands moving nervously together, parting, then joining.

'Victoria left a great many debts, Tyler too—they lived so well—they wanted so much! The house had to be sold—everything had to be sold—to pay their creditors. No one ever knew that either. All that was left was Tyler's portion of the Golden Gate—fifty-one per cent, enough to give him the controlling interest. He willed that right to his daughter . . . to little Eden, to be claimed on her eighteenth birthday. Tyler's partner agreed to run the Golden Gate for her—her share of the profits were to pay for her years at Miss Phelbert's.'

Lenore cast skittish eyes over her shoulder, hunching her body as if in fear, and her voice dropped again to that dry whisper. 'No one is supposed to know that—to ever know that!' She shook her head. 'Poor little Eden . . . poor little girl . . . she's been gone for so many years . . .'

The woman pivoted suddenly, the wispy folds of her négligé floating about her frail form. That vague hand came again across her forehead. 'But you're Eden!

You've grown up—you've come home!' She pressed her hands to her lips, whispering frenziedly from behind interlaced fingers. 'You weren't to know—you weren't ever to know—'

With horror Eden watched as Lenore's emaciated body began to shake uncontrollably, as if from a violent chill. Swaying as she stood, she wrapped her arms around her sunken chest and collapsed on to the *chaise*.

'Why doesn't Chang come with my medicine! It gets so bad—so bad when I don't have my medicine—Chang!'

At this long, pathetic wail of relief, Eden jerked her head to the doorway to see once again the noiseless Oriental standing there, sleeves flowing long over his hands. Without a word he came to Lenore and took her arm, his round yellow face devoid of expression.

Docile as a child, the woman went with the servant. She had forgotten Eden, forgotten her memories—forgotten everything but her medicine. Kneeling motionless, Eden listened to the piteous whimpers echo down the hall.

'I know I shouldn't have run away, Chang, I know it was wrong of me . . . Thank you for finding me—for coming after me. You know how bad it gets when I don't have my medicine . . . You know how much I need you . . .'

The voice grew fainter, and fainter still, and then a door shut softly.

Stiffly Eden came to her feet. Moving like an old woman, she walked to her door and shut it, and leaned there a moment.

'Get it straight, Miss Cortland, it's this cheap saloon that's kept you living like a lady!'

A voice, heavy and deep, had sounded suddenly in the room. No, no, the voice was only in her brain . . .

And as if to escape that voice, Eden began a restive pacing, moving like a caged animal from the canopied bed to the velvet-hung windows, from the marble-topped mantel to the golden handled dresser. Up and down, up and down, marking off a room a world away from the spartan quarters she d seen last night.

'You're no different from any of those girls on the stage or serving drinks—you both make your living off the Golden Gate!'

Eden began to run, feet sinking frantically into the deep white carpet. Faster and faster yet she went, until she was flushed and panting and there was an ache in her side.

'I thought you said you weren't afraid of anything. Well, why don't you admit it—you're afraid to face the truth.'

The truth.

Rigid as a pointer Eden drew up. Stock still she stood. Her heavy breathing filled the room. She pressed her palms to her temples to try and stop their frantic throbbing, but her brain would not be still—the words would not go away.

It was true. It was true. And with the truth came the destruction of her life. Eden Cortland's past—and her future—lay like rubble around her feet. But from the wreckage one inescapable fact had emerged.

That great gilded palace, that swirling kaleidoscope of noise and colour was now hers. And she must confront it.

She did not know what she would do when she got to the Golden Gate. She only knew she had to go.

Eden whirled around. In the tall secretary she found paper and quilled pen. Swiftly she wrote a note.

She had learned the secret of her past—she must go now where she could make some sense of that secret. That past. Julius must not follow her.

Like a golden spider her guardian had spun a web of wealth around her, and at the thought of breaking that web, a strange chill went down her spine. But of that —and a thousand other things—she must not think.

She must only act. Her resolve was too fragile a thing to bear scrutiny. Any probing and her courage might snap in two.

Eden began to run again, but this time her steps knew a pattern, her hands held a plan. From the huge closet she grabbed two of the valises the maid had stored there. Feverishly she began pulling open dresser drawers, snatching out handfuls of neatly folded clothes, throwing them carelessly into the suitcases.

She'd never dressed herself without aid, but to awaken a maid would be to reveal her intent. And so she managed her own toilette, fumbling with the frontal stays on her wasp-waisted corset, fingers struggling to fasten the row of pearl buttons that ran the length of her lace shirtwaist, awkwardly jerking at the grey silk travelling suit.

She'd never dressed her own hair, either, but she managed that too, braiding it, then winding the thick ropes atop her head.

The house was still, only the scullery maid stirred sleepily in the kitchen, but the plush carpeting concealed the sound of Eden's descent of the stairs. A valise in either hand, she pushed with her back against the heavy front door, went swiftly down the long flight of marble steps and through the iron fence to the street.

The sky was just beginning to flush pink with the dawn and the early morning air was new-minted and clear, fresh with the scent of flowers. Eden took several gulping breaths, filling her lungs.

A single drayman inhabited the street and, high French heels tapping a rapid staccato against the pavement, Eden ran towards him.

'Please, sir! Please stop!'

The driver clicked to his swaybacked horse and pulled rein, his leathery little face wrinkling up in wonder as he stared at this well-dressed and obviously well-bred young lady running wildly down Nob Hill at dawn.

Panting from the unaccustomed exertion, Eden stumbled over her words. 'Do you—do you know where the Golden Gate saloon is?'

In astonished reply the man's bushy white eyebrows lifted, his lips parted, the large-bowled pipe stuck between his teeth in imminent danger of falling out. Dumbly he nodded.

'Will you take me there?'

Goggle-eyed, the driver removed his pipe. 'That's no place for a lady.'

'I know all about that,' Eden answered him impatiently. 'Please—I have to get there!'

Muttering, the man shrugged and leapt to the ground. 'I hope you know what you're doing.'

He hefted Eden's valises atop the crates of sweet smelling fruits and vegetables, then reached out a hand to help her up. Once again he clambered aboard his wobbly-wheeled cart and to the touch of the switch the old horse plodded slowly forward and down the steep street.

Wedged between the boxes, Eden felt the bruises of the night before with every jolt—remembered the man who had inflicted them.

A warning bell went off in her mind. She must not think. She must not remember. She must not think of Chance Mallory—she must not remember his last words to her.

But like a ghost that would not be laid to rest his presence hovered over her. Rough, powerful, violent, he had come to symbolise the maelstrom into which she was plunging—and from which there might be no road back.

Cold fear, buried beneath her surface determination, stirred. Eden dug her nails into her gloved palms, clenching her fists.

Must not think. Must not think.

Ever downward the horse toiled, the wagon bumping along behind, and as they went Eden Cortland watched the world as she knew it disappear. The towering mansions with their terraced gardens and gabled roofs gave way to the solid stone houses of the middle class, these in turn giving over to clapboard apartment houses. Next came the warehouses and hardware stores and harness shops. And finally that tightly packed bit of hell called the Barbary Coast.

But the streets that had simmered like the devil's cauldron the night before were deceptively quiet that morning, as if resting—waiting—for the bewitching hour to flame into life once more.

The one-storey wooden wine dens and beer groggeries with their peeling paint and broken windows, seemed harmless in the bright sunlight. The red lights that marked the parlour houses were dimmed, the red shades drawn. The small gambling houses were shuttered.

The drayman reined in before the three-storey brick walls of the Golden Gate and quickly Eden climbed down and retrieved her suitcases.

'Good luck, Miss,' the little driver said mournfully, 'whatever it is you're after.' He clucked to the horse. 'Giddap.'

The electric lights that blazed the saloon's name after sundown sparked no fire now, the faint strains of a melancholy piano the only sign of life. For an instant Eden hesitated, listening to the plaintive tune. Even now she knew she might bolt and run. But she didn't. Setting one shoulder against the swinging doors, she pushed them open.

It was cool and dim within, the windows bolted and draped, and it took a moment for Eden's eyes to become accustomed to the gloom. The chairs were atop the tables, two men in overalls and rough shirts were cleaning the floor, while a third, a bucket of soapy water at hand, was scrubbing the stage.

A man in his shirtsleeves was behind the piano, his sad song switching abruptly to the Mississippi Rag. The only other person present was a woman dealing out a game of solitaire against one of the green baize tables. At Eden's entrance she collected the deck with a snap and stood.

She was obviously corsetless beneath her bright green kimono, with a magnificent bosom and ample hips that swayed languidly as she strolled forward. Though it was still morning, she was elaborately rouged and powdered —but it was her hair that drew Eden's eyes.

Flowing freely over her shoulders it was a bright, blazing red—too red to be real—and though 'women who had done something to their hair' had been a prime topic of late night conversation at Miss Phelbert's, Eden had never seen one close up. That is, not until now.

The woman grinned, obviously not at all disturbed by Eden's gaping stare, and her wide smile cut through the heavy paint to make her harsh-featured face seem a little less hard, a little younger. Making Eden's jaw drop still further, she pulled out a cigar and a match from her pocket and lit up.

'Name's Butterfly Sloan, honey. Can I do something for you?'

With difficulty, Eden collected herself. 'I—I'd like to see the manager.'

'That so?' Butterfly drew in deeply on the cigar and blew out a series of billowing black smoke rings. 'Looking for a job are ya?'

'No—I—'

'Don't be shy, sweetie. You're not the kind we usually hire in here and that's the truth, but put on a little paint, loosen up your hair and you just might have possibilities.'

'I'm not looking for a job,' Eden said stiffly. 'I just want to see the manager.'

Shrugging, Butterfly turned. 'Suit yourself, honey. The Boss is upstairs—follow me.'

Heavy hips swinging languorously, Butterfly led the way to the gilded stairway and up, gesturing to the rows of closed doors opening from the second floor landing. 'Us girls roost up here—no gentlemen allowed. The Boss runs a real respectable place, no honky-tonkying.'

As they mounted the second flight of stairs and started down the narrow hall, memories pressed against Eden like weights. *Don't think—mustn't think—*

Butterfly stopped before a closed door, from behind

which came a curious slapping sound and a man's hard
grunts. 'The Boss used to be bare-knuckle champ of the
whole waterfront,' the redhead explained. 'He still
works out regular every morning. Comes in real handy,
running this place.' She rapped on the door. 'There's a
gal—' Butterfly glanced at Eden and grinned, 'I mean a
lady to see ya.'

Butterfly turned, black smoke haloing around her
head. 'Don't let him cold deck ya, honey, the Boss can
be kinda fierce.' She winked, then sashayed down the
hall, her kimono dropping low to reveal a yellow butterfly tattooed on her right shoulder.

Eden gripped the doorknob. There was a cold dread
in the pit of her stomach, but behind the gauzy veil her
black, slanted eyes held a fierce glitter. She felt fear
—yet more.

Like the day she'd boarded the train to San Francisco,
like all those restless, dream-filled nights, a wild anticipation was rising within her. Quickly she opened the
door—and pulled up short. In a little gasp of disbelief
her breath escaped her lungs.

It was Chance Mallory who stood there.

CHAPTER
FOUR

HE WAS stripped to the waist, his back to her. With hard,
rapid movements right and left he was jabbing his fists
against a large leather bag suspended from the ceiling.

'You're the Boss?' Eden blurted out incredulously.

Fists raised, Mallory froze. 'Well, I'll be—' With a
new fury he began again to pummel the bag. 'I thought
I'd seen the last of Eden Cortland.'

'Why didn't you tell me everything last night?' Eden
rushed on, heedless of his words. 'Why didn't you tell me
I'm now the owner of the Golden Gate—and that you're
my partner?'

'What difference does it make?' His words exploded
in short, violent bursts, punctuated by the heavy sound
of his breathing. 'I told you everything I thought you
needed to know.'

'Yes, but I thought you were—' Eden caught herself
up sharply.

Chance wheeled around. His rugged face was
guarded, his chest and shoulders heaving. 'You thought
I was the hired thug maybe—or the handyman. You
didn't figure I was good enough to be Tyler Cortland's
partner.'

Eden didn't answer, flushing to the roots of her hair.
That was exactly what she had thought.

He let out his breath in a sardonic chuckle. 'Well, I
wasn't his partner—I never even met your father. I won

my share of the Golden Gate just three years ago, in the ring.' A corner of that hard mouth curled mockingly upward. 'What the devil are you doing here anyway? Was it the place you found so irresistible—or the people?'

'Neither.' Eden hesitated. 'It was something you said that made me return—'

His eyes narrowed. In silence he waited for her to finish. But Eden was finding it difficult to go on.

She had seen half-clad men before, on the beach, boating, but there was something oddly disturbing about the sight of Chance Mallory's naked torso—rock hard, matted with burnished hair, the heavy muscles spangled with sweat. Something that made speech difficult— something that made the small room seem airless and far too warm.

Eden lifted her veil, took a breath, and pushed herself on. 'You—you started me on the road to the truth—' She faltered. 'And when I knew the truth, I also knew I couldn't go on living a lie. I had to come back—I have to find my place—'

'I can tell you your place,' Mallory returned tersely, 'and it's not here.'

Sharply he turned back to the bag, attacking it with a barrage of hard, fast blows. Half-mesmerised by the furious rhythm of his fists, Eden watched him. She could not tear her eyes from him, from the powerful swell of his arms, from his tapering waist, from the glistening, fluid muscles of his back.

She did not register the sudden silence of the bag, did not notice he had turned his head and was staring at her. It was the inner pressure of his eyes that drove up her head.

Hands on his hips, Mallory swung around. Like some predatory animal that paralyses its quarry with the force of its gaze—the threat of attack—he held her motionless.

Last night Eden had felt the power of Chance Mallory's masculinity across a room crowded with people. Last night it had been a leashed force, straining at the bars—but now it had broken its bonds and was raging free. Now they were alone.

For an instant Eden held rooted—and then she turned and fled.

Quickly Chance came after her. He stretched out an arm, slamming the door shut just as she reached it, blocking her escape. A soundless cry caught in Eden's throat. Slowly she turned to face him, and as she did, he brought up his other hand against the door.

'What's your hurry, Miss Cortland?' Through half-lidded eyes he looked down at her, and his voice was lazy with insult. Deliberately he leaned close. 'Feeling a little less like a lady?'

Eden turned her head hard against the wooden planking. A terrible heat was washing over her in waves, she felt as if she were fighting for air.

With the rising and falling of every breath his chest grazed her breasts, yet he pressed closer still, his body singeing her skin through the layers of clothes—his very touch starting the perspiration across her bodice, along her back.

Eden felt a fire deep inside, melting her, throbbing like an ache—pleasuring her even as it shamed her.

Desperately she clasped her hands behind her and dug them into the small of her back, as if to goad herself into courage. But when she spoke her low voice was shaking.

'Let me go—you—barbarian!'

Mallory reared back, roaring with laughter, and the mocking sound of it turned Eden scarlet and then white.

'You don't have to worry, Miss Cortland, women like you have never held much attraction for me.' He picked up a towel from the back of a chair and began to wipe off his arms and chest with measured strokes. 'And now that you're done slumming, you can go back where you belong.'

Eden righted her hat, her skirt. A new determination was surging through her, given life by Mallory's jeering words, his gibing laughter. Why she had come and what she must do were suddenly clear.

'Mr Mallory, this is where I belong and this is where I intend to stay.'

He slung the towel around his neck. 'And just what do you plan on doing here?'

'I plan on running the Golden Gate!' Triumphantly Eden went on. 'May I remind you that while you own but forty-nine per cent of this establishment, I own fifty-one per cent. Legally, I have the right to do whatever I please here!'

Chance's eyes hardened to gun metal, blazing with an inward fire that made his clenched jaw tremble. With a violence that made Eden start, he jerked open the door.

'Ah Wan!' he bellowed into the hall, a vein throbbing in his temple, 'Ah Wan!'

Waves of rapid Chinese sounded up the stairs, growing ever louder until a tiny Oriental man, pigtail bobbing against his back, dashed into the room. He wore a blue linen tunic and trousers, and his eyes were like raisins in his sallow, wrinkled face. For one so incredibly wrinkled, his speed was remarkable.

'Whatchee want, Mr Boss?'

Savagely Mallory jerked his head towards Eden. 'I want you to show Miss Cortland to the second floor suite. She's running the place now—she's your new boss. You'll be taking care of her from now on.'

'Oh, no! Oh, no!' Vehemently Ah Wan shook his head. 'Me no wantee gel boss! Oh, no!'

In another burst of jangling Chinese the Oriental continued his protests, head waggling, hands gesticulating wildly, but Mallory's flat voice cut through the torrent.

'Quit your complaining and get going.'

'Hmph!' The little man shook his head so hard his pigtail bounced. Grim disapproval in his black, currant eyes, he beckoned to Eden, then sped away, still muttering ferociously.

Eden lifted her head. Every line of her body was erect with quiet grace and her words held a fine superiority.

'I quite understand your rudeness, Mr Mallory, you were obviously bred to it. But I hope you will understand when I say it in no way affects me. You see, I was bred to ignore the ill manners of the lower classes.'

And with an elegance even Harriet Phelbert would have approved, Eden sailed through the door and into the hall—and was rewarded by the sound of a bare fist slamming hard into the leather bag.

It was the music that awakened Eden. For a moment she lay still in the darkness, listening to the raucous ragtime wail. Would she ever grow used to it?

She could see the lights of the Barbary Coast from her bed, winking up and down the streets with tawdry brightness, pushing against the night, challenging the fog. The fog . . .

She'd watched that fog roll in. Silent, motionless, she'd stood, staring out the window as, mumbling in an undertone of clamorous Chinese, Ah Wan had laid away her clothes. She'd ignored the tray of food he'd brought her, ignored the spicy scent of the tea he'd poured.

Even after he'd gone she'd stood there, still silent, still motionless, watching mist devour the streets one by one, listening to the moaning of the boat whistles, the deep, throaty voices of the foghorns, the clang of the trolley bells. Giving in to the thoughts she'd fought back all day . . .

Finally, when her eyes were glazed with weariness, her legs twitching from fatigue, her brain deadened with thought, she'd fallen fully-clothed on the bed and found refuge in a deep, dreamless slumber.

But the eruption of noise and music below—outside —had yanked her back to reality, driven away the sweet forgetfulness of sleep.

Stiffly Eden pushed herself to one elbow, her body aching from the cramped position in which she'd spent the last several hours. She fumbled across the bedside table for the lamp chain and the room sprang into life.

The massive brass bed stood against one wall, a large walnut desk against the other. The floors were covered with fur rugs, the windows hung with dark green drapes. In a grouping before the hearth several deep uphol-stered chairs flanked a squat table on which rested a cigar box, and a carafe and glasses. A brass spittoon stood in the corner.

The dressing-room opened to one side, furnished with

a heavy walnut wardrobe and matching bureau. Perched on claw feet was a deep bath tub with brass fittings.

It was a man's room, tailored to a man's needs, spacious, uncluttered—and Eden wondered fleetingly why Chance Mallory preferred the bare quarters on the third floor.

Chance Mallory. Eden buried her face in the pillow, writhing inside, the memory of those fine, brave things she'd said to him that morning whirling and whirling around inside her brain. All of them empty promises.

She knew Mallory was waiting for her—waiting in that garish arena below to watch the lions devour her whole. Well, he would have to wait. She couldn't go down—she wouldn't. If her afternoon's thoughts had anything clear it was that. She couldn't do it. She would stay here tonight—maybe forever.

Quickly Eden stood and ran to the window, drawing the curtains across the sights and sounds of the Barbary Coast. With a mad haste, as if in time to the pounding music, she began unbuttoning her wrinkled skirt. She must hurry—hurry—back to the sanctuary of bed and darkness and blessed sleep, away from the unseen but deeply felt dangers below.

So frenzied was she, so intent, and so loud was the music, she didn't hear the doorknob turn—didn't hear the door swing open.

She slipped out of her suit, then unfastened her shirtwaist, mounding them haphazardly on a chair. She stepped out of the twin taffeta petticoats, tossing both atop the pile. Next came the corset.

Standing in smocked chemise and ruffled drawers to the knee, she yanked the pins from her hair, and the thick, black waves fell below her waist.

'You put on quite a show, Miss Cortland, but you're a little scrawny for our tastes down here.'

Eden whirled around, too stunned to speak at the sight of Chance Mallory. He had a casual shoulder propped against the doorjamb, his sleeves rolled above the elbow to reveal muscular forearms, his shirt open at the neck to show the thatch of burnished hair at the base of his strong throat.

Instinctively Eden's hand went to her breast, covered from his eyes solely by a panel of Venetian lace. At the obvious gesture Mallory laughed aloud. With that deliberate tread, he came forward.

'I have something for you.' He pulled a small pistol from his pocket and held it out to her. 'If you're going to stay here, keep this by the bed.'

Revulsion tingling across her scalp, Eden cringed away from the gun. Like the sting of a gnat, the very idea of the weapon seemed to bite at her, intensifying her fear.

But was her fear of this place—or of the man before her?

Chance Mallory and the Barbary Coast—they had become one in her mind, too violent, too full of life. Too near. She took a step backward and her voice quivered. 'I—I don't want the gun. Now please go. I'm not accustomed to receiving men—unclothed.'

Chance ran one hand consideringly over his hard jaw. As he had on the previous night, he let his eyes roam her. But this time there was a curiously penetrating quality to his narrowed glance—as if he were slowly stripping her bare.

Piece by piece Eden felt her garments fall beneath his gaze. The chemise, the pantalettes, the white silk stockings. The pit of her stomach dropped away. She was hot and cold—a rushing flood of warmth left her limp, her skin burning like dry ice.

His eyes came again to her face, his voice gibingly soft. 'I'd say you have a layer or two left.'

Chance nodded to the pile of clothes on the chair. 'I always wondered why ladies bothered with so much folderol—the women on the Barbary Coast are much more practical. Their clothes are far easier to get on—' one side of his mouth slanted insolently up, an eyebrow lifted insinuatingly, 'and off.'

Eden choked on her rage, her anger—at him, at herself—spilling over. 'Get out! Get out this instant or I'll—'

'Or you'll what?' he asked pointedly. 'Call the owner?' His face tightened into grim lines. 'You might have the legal right to stay here, Miss Cortland, but it's obvious you don't have the guts.'

Eden stared at him, defenceless against his lethal words. He'd found her out—brought her up short against her shame.

It was her own skulking fear that had stripped her of her dignity, robbed her of her ladylike veneer—sent her retreating into the darkness like a frightened animal cowering in its lair. She had decided to come to the Barbary Coast. Now she must accept the consequences of her action—or forever know herself as a coward. And Chance Mallory would know, too.

Slowly Eden came towards him and reached for the gun. The touch of his hand seemed to communicate something of his strength to her, the fierce blue eyes driving some of his mettle into her very soul.

'Thank you for the gift,' she said evenly.

He turned and started again for the door, tossing

careless words over his shoulder. 'It's a single shot derringer, so aim carefully.'

'Mr Mallory—' Eden brought up her other hand to grip the pistol, the feel of the hard steel seeming to help her rally her forces. 'Please know that I won't be so foolish a second time—from now on I'll keep my door locked.'

Chance stopped and shot her a long, cool look and his voice was very soft. 'If I wanted to get into your bedroom—' he flexed his hands into fists, 'it would take more than a locked door to keep me out.'

CHAPTER
FIVE

THE MUSIC stopped. The roulette wheel ceased spinning.
The dice cage rattled to a halt. Silence filled the Golden
Gate.

Every head swivelled around, every glance turned
upward, all attention focused on the slender girl coming
slowly down the stairs.

Deep within, Eden felt the pressure of those eyes.

Was it Ah Wan who had spread the news of a Nob Hill
lady taking over the Golden Gate? Did it matter? They
all knew—and they all waited. What would she do?
Would she survive? As thick and as real as the blue-
hazed curtain of smoke, their suspicion hung in the air.

One man only held apart. Both elbows resting on the
bar, Chance Mallory stood with one leg bent, a hand
around a glass. Like a spectator at a play in which he had
lost interest, he looked deliberately away.

Yet for all that studied indifference, Eden could see
the muscle twitching in his cheek, could feel his silent
challenge. As sharp as steel, his hostility struck at her
—roused her. She gripped the banister and the deep,
rich timbre of her voice reverberated across the room.

'Perhaps some of you think it strange that I've taken
over the Golden Gate, but I've come here because it's
my right—'

Her hand sliding nervously up and down the polished
wood, Eden hesitated. Still wary, the crowd watched

her, and into that unnatural hush, Chance Mallory's voice fell gibingly.

'Go on, Miss Cortland, we're all waiting.'

Long, tough body still slouched against the bar, he swung carelessly around to lift an expectant eyebrow —and at that, Eden plunged on.

'What I want to say is—'

She paused and licked her lips and from the corner of one eye, saw Chance lift his glass as if in mocking tribute. He drained it, then wiped his mouth on the back of one hand and grinned at her.

In blind determination, Eden struck out again. 'What I want to say is—'

She stopped dead. Her mind was blank—emptied by Chance Mallory's insolence.

'What she wants to say,' Butterfly Sloan bellowed, 'is that the next round is on the house! So drink up, gents!'

A resounding cheer met Butterfly's words. The music started anew, brighter even than before, the chatter was brisker, the laughter bawdier. For the moment Eden Cortland was forgotten.

In a rush of limp relief, Eden let out her breath. She had weathered the first storm. Quickly she forced her feet down the final steps and came to Butterfly's side.

'Thank you,' Eden said simply. 'That was kind of you.'

Butterfly grinned. 'Got to keep the customers happy. They always lay down more loot if they've had a free snort.' She drew on her cigar and tossed her red head towards the gaming tables. 'Why don't you drop around tonight and watch me work—you might as well start learning the ropes.'

Eden blinked. 'You're a—dealer?'

'Best faro dealer west of the Mississippi!' Butterfly responded with emphatic pride. She dug an elbow into the ribs of the man next to her. 'I'm quicker than greased lightning with the faro box, ain't I, Roy?'

The man bobbed his bald head. 'You sure are, Butterfly—and honest, too!'

'So you're the new owner of this joint, huh?'

Eden tightened at the shrill words that echoed spitefully behind her. Head up, she came stiffly around to confront the speaker—a barmaid with lacquered blonde hair and a spectacular figure that strained at the seams of her purple spangled gown.

'Mind your own business, Lily,' Butterfly said pointedly, but the girl merely made a face at her over one shoulder.

Hands on her hips, Lily looked back to Eden, and her heavily painted lips pursed into a taunting line. 'Tell me, Miss Eden Cortland from Nob Hill, how does it feel to be a highfalutin' lady?'

Eden lifted one black eyebrow and in her bare glance was the kind of frozen contempt she had learned so well at Miss Phelbert's. 'I wouldn't know,' she answered in dulcet tones, 'for, unlike yourself, I have never *not* been a lady.'

Lily bristled, obviously ready to explode into violent words, but at that moment Chance Mallory came up behind her and caught one plump arm.

'Simmer down, Lil.'

He pulled the blonde close, and her anger immediately forgotten, Lily snuggled up against him, bridling with pleasure. Over her spun-sugar hair, Chance gave Eden a sharp, half-lidded look.

'I happen to know—from personal observation—that underneath all her fine feathers, a lady's not much different from a barmaid.' He glanced at Eden's breasts, then casually stroked a hand across the wide expanse of Lily's bosom and his voice was wry. 'Except maybe there's a little less of her.'

Lily erupted into a tremolo of high-pitched giggles, her head nestling naturally into the curve of Chance's shoulder. Dropping his hand to her waist, he led her away.

A slow rage began to burn in Eden's brain. Or was it the unexpected—unwanted—flare of jealousy that seared her? Sharply, she turned on her heel.

Butterfly following, Eden marched to the bar and to the bartender's amazement and the customer's consternation, seized the drink that had just been poured and downed it in a gulp.

In a kind of grim toast of her own, she lifted the emptied glass towards Chance Mallory's retreating back. 'I don't care what he says or what he does,' she gasped out, her mouth still scorched from the whisky, 'I'm not leaving!'

But her brave declaration ended in a choking cough. Chuckling, Butterfly thumped her helpfully on the back.

'I have a feeling, you're going to do just fine, honey, just fine.'

'Beggin' yer pardon, Miss Eden—'

A bear of a man in a chequered suit stood before her. His brown hair was parted rigorously in the middle and flattened to either side, perched atop his well-waxed head was a derby. Shyly he took it off, twisting it around and around in ham-sized hands as he spoke. 'The Boss said you were runnin' the place now.'

'Honey, meet Seamus Muldoon,' Butterfly gave his cheek an affectionate tweak. 'Seamus has the hardest head and the biggest heart on the waterfront—he kind of looks after things around here.'

Eden extended her hand. 'I'm pleased to meet you, Mr Muldoon.'

Taking her proffered hand in a blood-congealing grip, Seamus pumped it enthusiastically. 'Likewise!'

Seamus Muldoon had a broad, flat face and several missing teeth, and his three-tiered nose looked as if it had been broken and reset so many times that the original shape had long ago been forgotten. But there was an obvious sincerity in his puppy dog eyes and an eagerness in his wide grin that Eden couldn't help responding to. Warmly she returned his smile—even as she wondered if she'd ever have the use of her hand again.

'Anything going on tonight, Seamus?' Butterfly asked, blowing smoke rings ceilingward.

'Could be.' The chequered giant extended his derby towards a band of roistering sailors. 'The crew from the *Sea Star* just hove in—one of the girls tipped me off that Cap'n Dagget's carryin' a gun and some of the others are packin' shivs.'

'Knives,' Butterfly explained to Eden. She gave a snort. 'That rotten bunch! They know there's a house rule against customers carrying weapons.'

Seamus put on his derby. 'Don't worry, Miss Eden, I'll take care of it. The Boss told me you'd be needin' help—and plenty of it! He said you'd be like a babe in the woods and I should stick closer than glue—and that's what I aim to do!'

'Oh, he did, did he?' Eden flared. 'Well, I'm sorry to

disappoint you and Mr Mallory, Seamus, but I can look after myself!'

From under lowered lashes, Eden cast a look at the sailors. Then swiftly—uneasily—she glanced away, and with a bravado she was far from feeling went briskly on, 'I was taught out East that all men respond to reason —even men like that! I'll simply talk to them—ask them to lay down their weapons.'

Seamus and Butterfly exchanged an eloquent look.

'Honey,' the redhead began carefully, 'I know you mean well, but Dagget and his crew are pretty rough.' She laid a hand on Eden's arm. 'At least let me tag along with you.'

Eden shook off the restraining hand. 'Thank you, but no,' she said firmly. 'You've helped me enought tonight, Butterfly. The Golden Gate is my responsibility now.'

Purposefully Eden started through the crowd. That it was the goad of Chance Mallory's insolence that urged her on, she knew. Every step was somehow a rebuttal to his contempt.

The sailors were packed three deep before the roulette wheel, but as she came towards them, they stopped their gambling and stared. Eden's mouth was cotton-dry, her face flushed. Her first attempt at speech produced nothing but a croak. The men snickered at the sound. She gulped and tried again.

'Pardon me—'

A heavy man with a drooping black moustache and a wad of tobacco distending his cheek turned from the gaming table to face her. He was dressed as were the others—striped sweater, pea jacket, belled trousers, but their ready deference to him proclaimed him the leader.

'Well, well, well,' small, close-set eyes gleamed in his

swarthy face as he ran both hands over the black hair that hung in oily waves to his shoulders. 'The Golden Gate didn't have anything like this the last time we put in, did it, boys?'

At that the men nudged one another, grinning lewdly. Almost as if at a prearranged signal, they moved in around her.

Bolt and run, Eden's brain was telling her, but the memory of Chance Mallory's gibes held her firm. 'Please,' she said resolutely, 'may I have a word with you—'

The monkey-faced leader spat out a stream of tobacco juice, narrowly missing Eden's skirts. 'You can say anything you like, little lady, but why not come closer?'

He shot out long arms and pulled her roughly towards him, his fat, oily fingers tangling in her hair. Gasping, Eden struggled against him, the bile of nausea rising in her stomach as the rank odour of his unwashed flesh assailed her nostrils.

His thick lips brushed her own, sending a shudder of loathing through her, and with all her strength she shoved against him. Chuckling, he released her. But as Eden turned to flee, she found herself surrounded by the other sailors. Arms folded, they ringed her like a pack of wolves.

Senses sharpened by fear, Eden saw jeering faces, greedy eyes—all merging dizzyingly with the glitter of the Golden Gate. Just beyond that hellish circle, she saw Butterfly, her harsh-featured face creased in anguish.

She saw Chance Mallory.

There was nothing on his rough-hewn face, nothing in the steely eyes. One corded forearm was stretched taut over Seamus Muldoon's broad chest—as if to prevent him from aiding her.

Well, Eden Cortland didn't need anyone's help, she decided defiantly. She stiffened her spine, squared her shoulders. Swiftly, she darted forward—but the sailors closed ranks against her.

Again she tried to break free—and again and again, until her breathing was quick and shallow and her eyes were wild. But each time the circle grew smaller.

It was a children's game they were playing, but in deadly earnest, and the pent-up lust of their months at sea was plain on their faces.

One of the men spun her off her feet and swung her into his arms, then tossed her carelessly to a comrade. From one to the other Eden was tumbled, the men roaring with laughter as her blouse was torn from her shoulder, her skirts flying high to give a flashing display of leg and thigh.

Half-blinded by the black hair streaming loose from its pins, Eden tried to strike out at them, clawing at their faces, but her puny efforts only brought forth fresh gales of laughter.

Abruptly the wild game came to a halt. In the sudden silence Eden heard hard, heavy words.

'Give me the girl, Dagget.'

Eden tossed her head, shaking the hair from her eyes. Breast heaving with fear and exertion, her words came out in short, panting bursts. 'I don't need your help, Mr Mallory—I can handle this alone!'

A small, tight smile curved Chance's lips sardonically downward. 'I can see how well you're handling things.' His voice sharpened, softened, 'Give me the girl, Dagget,' he repeated.

In reply the swarthy sailor nodded to the man holding Eden. Pell-mell she was tossed into Chance's arms.

Without a glance at her, Chance thrust her behind him. Barely standing erect, Eden had to resist the temptation to bury her head against his strong back.

'The girl means that much to you, eh, Mallory?' Dagget asked, grinning.

'The girl means nothing to me,' Chance answered with vicious clarity. 'But the Golden Gate does and I don't want to see you or any of your men in here again. Now get out.'

'We'll go,' Dagget said in a low voice. Once again he ran both hands over his oily black hair and with his mouth thinned to an ugly line. 'We'll go—' He pulled a derringer from his belt. 'But not before we leave you something to remember us by!'

Chance shoved Eden to the floor, she felt the weight of his body atop hers. A shot rang out, so close overhead the whining shriek seemed to scream in her brain. The bullet smashed into the long mirror behind the bar, the glass collapsing in a jangling spray.

Chance leapt to his feet and lunged for Dagget. Seizing the sailor by the scruff of the neck, he threw him across the bar with a force that sent him spinning over the polished wood like a top.

Turning, Chance's grip closed about Eden's wrist. He pulled her to her feet and dragged her across the floor, shoving her underneath one of the tables.

'Stay low,' he muttered, overturning a few chairs as a barricade, 'and keep out of sight. I know this place and these people—all hell is about to break loose.'

He swung around and into the crowd. Huddled behind her makeshift shelter, Eden stared in dazed disbelief at the fury erupting around her.

Their ready tempers ignited by the liquor's fire, inflamed by the fever of the gaming tables, the customers of the Golden Gate had responded to the sight and sound of violence with reckless delight.

Dozens of fights were raging across the gilded room, on the stage, up and down the stairs. The air was thick with flying fists, flying crockery.

Eden saw windows smashed, mirrors shattered. She saw men vaulting chairs and overturning tables, striking out at random—and without rancour—merely for the sheer joy of battle.

She saw the musicians dive behind the mahogany barricade of the bar, while the saloon girls waded happily into the mêlée, bashing one and sundry with anything they could get their hands on, plates, bottles, glasses.

She saw Seamus Muldoon using his head like a battering ram to butt down Dagget's men as if they were a field of ripe wheat. She saw Butterfly's red hair waving like a pennon as she rescued the portraits from the wall. When a bullnecked sailor with a gold ring in one ear grabbed her from behind for a kiss, she calmly crowned him with a picture and went on.

Eden saw Chance Mallory—straining her eyes across the room until she found him. His dark auburn hair was long and loose over his forehead and there was a rip in his linen shirt, a felled opponent at his feet. His arms were stretched out and in either hand he held a man helpless by the shirt front, trying vainly to restrain them from clobbering one another.

Stealthily one of Dagget's men was advancing on him from behind, a knife upraised.

'Chance!'

But Eden's warning cry fell soundlessly into the storm raging around them. In one compact movement she pushed upright, grabbed a bottle from the table and let it fly.

The bottle crashed into the back of the sailor's head shattering as it struck him. He pitched to the floor.

Eden stared at the sailor. She stared at her hands —white, pampered, useless hands that somehow tonight had found the courage to strike back—strike out— reclaim a little of her own.

For the first time in her life Eden felt a thrill of raw, savage pride surge through her. For the first time she felt strangely akin to these reckless, wild men and women of the Barbary Coast.

And then a series of sharp, shrill whistles pierced her consciousness. Quickly she lifted her head.

The fighting had stopped, the crowd falling back before a clutch of policemen. They wore hard round-topped helmets, and there were revolvers at their hips, badges glittering on their blue-belted frock coats.

The officer in the forefront shoved up to Chance. His double row of brass buttons was tarnished, his girth straining against his belt, and with a kind of brutal eagerness he was slapping his white gloved hand hard with his nightstick.

'Good evening, Sergeant Cross,' Chance said with venomous politeness and a malicious twist to his voice that mottled the policeman's face red with rage. 'And what brings you to the Golden Gate tonight?'

'You know damn well why I'm here, Mallory!' Cross spat out. 'You've been warned before about this kind of disturbance—and now I'm going to have the pleasure of running you in!'

Without conscious thought, Eden started forward —and at first she did not recognise the firm voice she heard as her own.

'I'm in charge of the Golden Gate now, Officer. If you arrest anybody, it will have to be me.'

The floor of the cell was slippery with green slime. The walls were stone, damp and clammy and dripping with moisture. A solitary dirty bulb hung from the ceiling, the single window was small and barred and high.

The single occupant was Eden.

The ride from the Golden Gate to the jailhouse in the filthy insect-infested police wagon had been a forever. Without a word a yawning officer had led her down a dark, dank corridor—and now, hands in her lap, feet flat on the floor, she sat stiffly on the cubicle's only chair.

She stared down at the tattered petticoat poking from beneath the rips in her silk skirt. She felt the chill wetness of the air against her skin, her shoulder left bare by the tear in her blouse. Her hands and face were dirty, her tongue was gritty. Her hair hung in disorderly snarls down her back.

What was it Miss Phelbert had told them again and again? 'A true lady looks like a lady no matter what circumstances she finds herself in.'

Well, Harriet Phelbert would be disappointed in her now.

And at that thought, Eden felt a near hysterical desire to laugh. Desperately she clapped a hand to her mouth. She must not give in to the blind panic that threatened her.

It lay in wait for her everywhere that terror, it oozed

down the walls, it hung in the mouldering air. If she gave in to it, it would consume her.

Abruptly Eden started. Her scalp tingled. Something was crawling over her feet.

Without moving her head, she shot a glance from the corner of her eye to see a rat, poised on the edge of her shoe. Boldly, blackly, his little eyes gleamed up at her.

Like a crazy woman Eden leapt to her feet, wrapping her arms so tightly about her, her breath congealed in her chest. Tears began to sear the corners of her eyes, and she squeezed her lids shut against them. If they started, they would never stop.

She was teetering on the brink now, fear threatening to overwhelm her.

How long—how long would they keep her here?

She didn't imagine they were too fastidious about justice in a Barbary Coast jail. Maybe she'd simply be left here to rot.

And maybe she deserved it—blundering from one mistake to the other, blindly rushing off to the Golden Gate, foolishly trying to reason with an animal like Dagget.

Trying to best Chance Mallory.

She hadn't looked at him as she'd been ushered out of the saloon and into the horse-drawn paddy wagon. She hadn't looked at anyone—but most of all she'd kept her eyes from Chance Mallory.

Yet, at the sudden thought of the man, a glimmer of courage flooded her darkened, feverish mind. Ill mannered he was, and crude and insolent, but he was also strong and fearless. He wouldn't let himself be held like this—if there was a way out he would find it. And so would she.

With new energy, Eden ran the few steps to the bars that fronted her cell, curling her hands around the cold iron. But even as she opened her mouth to summon an officer, she heard footsteps echoing down the hallway and a policeman emerged from the murky darkness. Striped in shadows, he fitted his key into the lock and the cell door swung open. He stepped inside, Eden retreated a pace.

His face was half hidden by the brim of his helmet and the sullen light did little to illuminate his features. But the heavy belly pushing against his tunic, the tarnished badge and buttons—the incessant beating of his nightstick upon his gloved palm—all marked him as the officer who had arrested her.

'We don't get many in this cell like you, Miss Cortland.'

There was an unpleasant suggestiveness to his voice and as he tipped back his helmet, Eden saw he was grinning. Quietly she moved her hand to the tear at her shoulder and pulled the flimsy material tightly together.

'How long—how long are you going to keep me here?'

'That all depends on you,' Cross said softly, smiling still, 'on how—friendly—you are. If you're a good girl and give me what I want, you could be out of here in an hour. If I have to use a little persuasion—' He paused and the dull pounding of his nightstick grew as loud and insistent as a drum roll, beating out his message. 'Well, that could take a whole lot longer.'

Eden blanched, revulsion filling her body, and at the disgust and horror on her face, Cross stopped smiling. His port-wine complexion went crimson in anger.

'So it's gonna be that way, huh?'

'You are a disgrace to your uniform,' Eden whispered, her voice shaking, 'and when I'm free I shall report you to the authorities—'

'When you're free,' Cross echoed her maliciously, an ugly look crossing her face, 'you won't be fit for much of anything.'

He took a step forward, swinging the nightstick as he came and Eden fell back before him. With dilated eyes she watched him hoist the stick high overhead.

But as he moved to bring the wood down against Eden's skull, his arm was seized from behind and Chance Mallory spun him around to drive a hard right to his jaw. Cross toppled backwards, his stick clattering to the floor beside him.

Across the still, blue body, Eden looked at Chance. Rock hard he stood, unmoving, the naked bulb casting stark shadows across the chiselled face, deepening the bitter lines around his mouth, flinging deep hollows beneath his steely eyes.

Eden clutched her hands to her throat. Beneath the white skin the blue veins were pulsing swiftly and her black eyes were enormous, glazed with delayed shock. The bravado that had sustained her through the tensions of that day, the terrors of the night, had melted away —and now she gave in to the tears she had disallowed before.

Now she gave way to the impulse she had denied herself at the Golden Gate. Now, as the room rocked and swayed around her, she struck out for the only certain oasis in this torment. Violently she cast herself against Chance.

Instantly she felt his body stiffen, but she didn't care. He was shelter and safety and she clung to him, her sobs as wild and racking as a child's.

He gripped her arms and held her away from him. 'Stop it,' he ordered her tersely, 'stop it!' He began to shake her—her head falling back, her black hair tumbling across her face, her torn blouse slipping from her shoulders.

Yet still the tears kept on, streaming down her face, her throat, her wrenching cries verging on hysteria.

Chance shot out a hand and struck her across the face.

The blow halted Eden's sobs in a choking gasp. She stared at him, the back of one hand pressed to her mouth, and the only sounds were her deep, shuddering breaths.

'I had to do that,' Chance said rigidly, spacing his words with a hardened deliberation that matched his narrowed gaze. 'I had to. Do you understand?'

Eden nodded once. The hand that thrust the hair from her face was trembling, a kind of hurt vulnerability still quivered at the corners of her mouth. Yet slowly the world was beginning to right itself.

Chance turned. 'Then let's go.'

The hallway was dimly lit and angled, but his long, light strides covered it quickly, leaving Eden panting in his wake. At the end of the corridor was a wide, heavy door, Chance swung it open to reveal a cart and horse awaiting them in the alley. Standing guard over both was Seamus Muldoon.

He came eagerly forward. 'Any problems, Boss?'

Chance shook his head. Negligently he caught Eden up, tossing her bodily atop the wagon. 'It helps when you know the layout.'

Still struggling to catch her breath, Eden stared down at him. 'You've been in there before?'

'Once or twice.' Chance ducked under the horse's neck, then swung up beside Eden, and the look he gave her was guarded. 'And not on visiting days. Sergeant Cross and I are old friends.'

Chance shifted his gaze. 'How about you, Seamus? Did you do as I said?'

'Sure, Boss. I bribed the guards just like you told me to—but I woulda rather busted a few heads!' He waggled his broken nose indignantly. 'Those bums! Draggin' off a fine lady like Miss Eden to a hole like this!'

'You've busted enough heads for one night,' Chance answered him dryly. 'I'd like you to stick around a while —just to make sure there's no slip-ups.'

Chance unwound the reins and the horse struggled into the mud, the wagon lurching, listing, righting itself. Both hands gripping hard to the planked seat, Eden hesitated a moment before she spoke.

'Will you be in trouble for striking a police officer? For taking me out of there?'

Chance laughed on a terse note. 'Sergeant Cross is hand in glove with all the corruption on the waterfront. Any city hall investigation of what happened tonight would only throw the rap square into his lap. Broken jaw or not, he'll keep quiet.'

Eden digested this in silence, then politely, primly, she said, 'Thank you for what you did tonight, Mr Mallory.'

For a moment there was a sharp silence, then into it Chance's voice fell with the bite of a blade.

'You said that just right, Miss Cortland, just the way one of the privileged class should speak to one of those on the bottom of the heap.'

It was nearly morning, but the gathering dawn was

silvered with fog, and in that dim half-light, Chance's face was set, locked away from her, his eyes fixed noncommittally on the street ahead. Had there been a bitterness in his words that went beyond anger—or had she only imagined it?

'It's true that I was raised in a world very different from yours,' Eden said quietly, yet with a steel-edged undercurrent to her words. 'But your world—whether I like it or not—is the only world I have now. The Golden Gate is all I have.'

'Thanks to Dagget and his crew there's not much left of the Golden Gate right now,' Chance said shortly. 'We'll either have to sell it—or close it down.'

'No!' Eden cried. 'Surely it can be repaired—'

'There's no money left in the till for repairs or anything else. I plough my share of the profits back into the business. Your share—' he flashed her a closed look, 'has been spent. Out East.'

At his hard words, Eden felt a shame that was almost physical pain. She tightened her hands until the knuckles went white.

'I know what happened tonight was my fault,' she said in a low voice. 'But I promise you—somehow I'll get the money we need.'

'And just how do you plan on doing that?' Chance glanced towards a tawdry red light blinking meaningfully in the early dawn and his teeth showed animal white in the jeering slash of a smile. 'Frankly I don't remember you having the right requirements for a lady of the evening.'

Fury rose hot and swift in Eden's heart—but summoning up the training of a lifetime, she battled it back. Carefully she answered him, 'I plan to borrow the money—from my guardian perhaps, or the bank—'

Chance drew rein so swiftly the horse reared back. There was a rolling anger burning in his face, smouldering in his eyes, and his voice shook with suppressed rage.

'There won't be a penny of your damn Nob Hill money spent on the Golden Gate! Is that clear?'

Eden recoiled. She was afraid of Chance Mallory at that moment, afraid of his latent strength—of the remembered power in that hard body.

'Is that clear,' he questioned again through set teeth, and the deadly quietness of his voice was the most frightening thing of all.

'Yes—yes.'

He took a breath, and the effort needed to recover his control was plain in the tenseness of his body. He averted his head, a light wind stirring the auburn hair across his forehead, at the nape of his neck. 'I've already decided how I'm going to get the money. I won the Golden Gate in the ring—I can save her the same way.'

Eden's black brows rushed together. 'There must be another way—'

'There is another way,' he shut her off harshly, 'the way of the rich—but that's your way, not mine.'

Suddenly, savagely, he turned to her and she felt the hardness of his fist against her throat, forcing up her chin, forcing her to face the dancing malice of his eyes.

'What's wrong, Miss Cortland, is the thought of a fight too barbaric for you? But then you called me a barbarian, didn't you? And maybe I am—maybe we all are here—'Restlessly his eyes raked her face, as if searching for something she could not give him. And behind those eyes—hidden in that mist-silvered face—was something she too wanted desperately, but which would forever be hidden from her. Something that held them both fixed and would lie like a barrier for all time between them.

Abruptly he pulled her close, and the roughness of his hands on her bare skin, the bruising thrust of his body were as she knew they would be. The downdrive of his kiss forced her lips apart and she tasted his mouth—she felt his chest hard against her breasts. She pressed her hands to his back, crushing him even closer, the blood beating up within her, answering him—demanding more.

And then into her reckless mind swept the past, bringing with it all that she was—all that she had been raised to be. In one wrench she tore herself from his arms.

Eyes glittering fiercely, Eden wiped the back of her hand across her mouth as if her lips had been touched by something unclean.

'I may be forced to live on the Barbary Coast, Mr Mallory, but I'll never understand your ways here—and I'll never like them!'

'Are you sure about that?' There was a diabolical gleam to his eyes, a brutal kind of mockery to his voice. 'You seemed to be enjoying yourself a moment ago.'

Eden's face went hot. She was sick with rage and humiliation and a strange, boiling disappointment that she could not understand—but which was the worst pain of all. He had won the moment—as he had won all the moments between them.

Chance lifted the reins and the horse bolted forward, throwing her hard against him. As if burnt, Eden jerked away.

But Chance Mallory did not seem to notice—or care.

CHAPTER
SIX

EDEN set down the heavy pail and dropped to her knees behind the other women, then she lifted out the sponge and began scrubbing. The hot, soapy water bit into the raw flesh of her hands, shooting pains stung her back, her knees. For weeks it had been so—the work, the pain.

First the red-handed, strong-backed charwomen hired from the waterfront had cleared away and carted off the forest of debris that littered the Golden Gate, the shattered glass, the smashed furniture. Then, as the men had fitted the new windows and hung the new mirrors, they'd scrubbed every square foot of the floor, each stair, all the walls, even the stage.

And with the women had laboured Eden.

Each night she'd lain in bed too exhausted to cry, muscles she had not known she possessed cramped and stiff, her hands chapped and blistered, the nails broken and split.

Each night Ah Wan had scolded her in vociferous Chinese as he forced her to swallow his pungent tea. Each night Butterfly, at Ah Wan's orders and with his special salve, had rubbed her down, shaking her red head as she did so.

'Honey, I just don't understand why you're putting yourself through this.'

'I told you, Butterfly,' Eden would answer her grimly,

'the Golden Gate is my responsibility now.'

It all had something to do with proving herself—but to whom? That she didn't know. Yet each day she'd come back. Each day she'd grown a little stronger, done a little more, until now she could lift her head on her aching neck and view with pride what she had helped accomplish.

The great gilded room was shiningly clean, glistening with new paint and old memories, just waiting for the music, the noise, the revelry that would make it complete. But once the Golden Gate was as it had been—to whom would it belong?

The answer depended on Chance Mallory—on his strength, the fury of his fists.

CHANCE MALLORY vs SYKES DAGGET!
GREATEST BARE-KNUCKLE BRAWL
OF THE CENTURY!
COME ONE—COME ALL!

The handbills announcing the contest had been plastered up and down San Francisco. Over cigars and brandy in the finer sporting clubs, over a round of beers in the lowliest saloons, the conversation was the same. The fight.

The backer was still unknown—a mysterious gentleman from Nob Hill some said. According to rumour, he'd scoured the city for an opponent with strength enough—and rage enough—to match Chance Mallory in the ring.

And in Sykes Dagget, it was agreed, he had found him.

It never occurred to Eden, however, that Chance

would not win. In her mind he was invincible—
invulnerable, an impenetrable puzzle of a man with his
jeering words and his bitter silences and his hard, tough
body. A body tuned to whipcord fitness in these past
weeks.

With grim-lipped intensity, Chance had lengthened
his hours at the bag, working out daily with sparring
partners. Every morning was devoted to road work.

And every morning, with a strange, inner intensity of
her own, Eden looked through the long windows of the
Golden Gate and watched him begin that daily run.
Watched him with a pleasure that was almost pain.

But why?

Certainly it was something the old Eden Cortland
would never have done. But the old Eden, that pampered creature of silk and lace who'd never lifted a hand
to help herself, had disappeared.

But if she was not what she had been, then who was
she? What was she? She did not belong on the Barbary
Coast—and she would not allow herself to belong on
Nob Hill. All she had was this limbo of backbreaking
work. So she forced herself on, trying to find in her
compulsive labour an escape from her thoughts, her
questions—a refuge from this dawning need that betrayed everything she'd been taught to be. The need for a
man who didn't need her.

It was obvious that Chance Mallory had no use for
her! He never noticed her. He never spoke to her. These
days Chance Mallory noticed no one—spoke to no
one—but Lily.

Lily, with the white blonde hair and luscious figure.
Lily, who hovered over him like a shadow. Lily, whom
Eden heard coming and going from that barren room on

the third floor too early in the morning and too late at night.

Eden took a breath and passed a hand over her forehead. She sank back on her heels, trying to ease her back and her mind for a moment—but the sudden glimpse she caught of herself in one of the long pier glasses brought her up short.

Her borrowed cotton dress hung like a rag on her body. Her face was shiny and streaked with dirt and her disorderly braids straggled one over each shoulder.

No, Chance Mallory never noticed her—and was it any wonder?

'I hear odds are running even on the fight,' Butterfly announced to the room at large as she sauntered down the stairs. In reply to Eden's smiled greeting the redhead winked and lit up her first cigar of the morning.

Seamus looked up from his breakfast of beer and chilli peppers and snorted. 'The Boss'll make mincemeat outta that chump! He's been trainin' like a bulldog.'

And as if to give weight to his words, Chance entered from his morning run. His high-necked black sweater was strained taut over his wide chest and square shoulders, and there was about his lean, corded body the powerful, controlled look of a finely trained stallion.

Her hunger to look her fill and her anger at herself mingling together, Eden wrenched her gaze from him. With vengeance she bent again to her work.

'My, my, Miss Cortland, don't you look charming this morning!'

At the shrill voice she knew too well, Eden tightened her back, tensed her muscles. Still poised on all fours, she looked up, but all she gave Lily was a curt nod.

'And your hair is so lovely!' Lily's rouged lips curved

into a candy-box smile. 'Did it take you much time to fix it that way?'

Eden met the malicious gaze squarely. 'I don't have to do much to my hair, Lily—you see, it's still my own colour.'

There was a titter from some of the other women at that, and a hearty guffaw from Butterfly. Swinging sharply around, Lily threw them a furious look. She tossed her head.

'Are you sayin' my hair ain't real?'

Eden lifted one black eyebrow in pointed emphasis. 'I'm saying it's as real as that beauty mark you paint on every morning.'

Lily's eyes bulged. She gripped her hands into fists, her heavy bosom rising and falling in rage. 'Why you little—I could tear your hair out for that!'

Eden sprang to her feet. Fierce, hot blood was pumping through her veins, burning in her heart. She was vitally alive, as she had been for those few minutes of the brawl—as she had been in Chance Mallory's arms. She swept up her chin and her head tilted proudly backwards.

'Then why don't you try!'

Spouting an oath, Lily hurled herself forward and knocked Eden to the floor. She fell on top of her, tugging with both hands on the black braids.

Eden gritted her teeth against the tearing pain in her scalp. She grabbed twin fistfuls of the sugar-blonde hair, yanking so hard Lily howled like a dog, releasing her grip. Eden struggled to her feet.

'Oh, no you don't!'

Lily scrambled to her knees and caught hold of one of Eden's legs. She came down in a heap. Arms and legs thrashing, clawing, kicking, biting, the two women went rolling over and over, first one on top, then the other.

The charwomen dropped their buckets. The barmaids rushed down the stairs. Whistling, clapping, the spectators formed a circle around the two combatants, Butterfly's encouraging calls soaring louder than all the rest.

'Thatta girl, honey! Give it to her!'

Eden was unconscious of the crowd, unaware of the bloody scratches on her face and arms, uncaring that her flimsy dress was torn to shreds. Something within her was screaming for revenge—for release—and it was that need that drove her on against the bigger, stronger girl. She couldn't give up—she wouldn't—and she fought like a terrier.

A bucket of cold, dirty water hit her square in the face, hit them both. Gasping and blinking, the two were hauled apart, Seamus seizing Lily in a hammerlock, Chance dropping the pail to swing Eden up and under one arm.

'Let me go! Let me go!'

With the fury of a child throwing a tantrum, Eden kicked and struggled. But Chance merely bore her silently away and up the stairs, and the laughter of the others followed them as they went, increasing her rage.

Chance pushed open the door of her suite and carried her to the bed. And then he dropped her. She fell flat on her stomach, landing so hard she bounced. Spitting venom, Eden spun around and up.

'How dare you treat me like this!'

'If you behave like a fishwife, you'll be treated like a fishwife,' Chance said calmly. 'Now, I suggest you take a bath. You look—and smell—like you need one.'

Speechless with anger, Eden stared at him, and in his

cool, casual face, she read all her tortures of the past
weeks—the suppressed desires, the frustrations, the
overwhelming fatigue. In one great wave they broke and
crashed over her and she grabbed the lamp from the
bedside table and hurled it at him.

Quick as a cat, Chance ducked away. The lamp
crashed against the wall behind him, the sound of it
hanging in the air like the echo after a bell has rung.

A dangerous light lit the steel of his eyes and the
hawkish thrust of his features was fiercer still in the new
gauntness of his face. A terse smile stretched his firm lips
tight. Without turning he kicked the door shut behind
him and in two strides he was across the room.

Eden fell at him, pummelling his chest with her fists,
but without effort he caught both her wrists and pushed
her backwards on the bed, pinning her arms above her
head. Deliberately he looked down at her and his face
was a dark, glittering void.

Eden's lips parted in fear—was it fear?

Though her mouth formed a plea for mercy no words
would come. Her silent cry was the cry of the soul and
her eyes held the blackness of night—the bewilderment
of her heart.

For a moment more Chance stared silently, then softly
he said, 'Take a word of advice from someone who
knows—never start a fight you can't finish.'

Abruptly he released her, jerking upright. He swung
around and started for the door—but one hand on the
knob, he halted.

'I don't want you at the fight tomorrow night,' he said
in a voice hoarse with control. 'Do you hear me? I don't
want you there.'

Eden sprang to her knees. Anger was jabbing at her

like a knife thrust, frantically she cast about for cruel words to hurl at him as she had hurled the lamp—words that would not miss their target, but would wound him—hurt him.

'You can't keep me away from that fight!' she cried. 'I want to be there—I want to see Sykes Dagget give you the thrashing of your life!'

Chance turned briefly back and there was a twitching rigidity to his lean profile, a bitter twist to his lips. 'Come then—and I hope Dagget doesn't disappoint you.'

A wispy fog hung over the harbour, the scattered lights of the ships at anchor occasionally breaking through the mist to glow like fireflies against the black water. The moon came and went, its shimmer falling intermittently across the sky. But the brightest lights on the waterfront that night were the torches that ringed the wharf.

A huge platform had been built at the water's edge, the centre portion of it raised and cordoned off. Within that square the fight would take place.

A fleet of small boats had been pulled in close and these were packed with spectators. The docks, too, were swarming with people, some clinging to the pilings, some perched atop rough planks set between two barrels.

Labourers stood elbow-to-elbow with top-hatted gentlemen from Nob Hill, fishermen and shopkeepers mixed with Orientals from Chinatown. There was an ample seasoning of saloon girls as well, and the torchlight reflected equably over painted faces, yellow faces, worn faces, all of them happily swigging beer and eating oysters, tossing the shells over their shoulders and into the water.

A banjo man and fiddler were whacking out ragtime melodies and their songs hung thickly in the humid air, blending happily with the unceasing stir and buzz of the crowd.

Stepping quickly, Eden followed the bright flame of Butterfly's dress—the same hue as her hair—through the ranks to where Seamus stood beckoning to them. His burly body hovered protectively over the two barrels he had saved in the front row, he was shorn of his derby and chequered coat, his shirt sleeves rolled above the elbow. Across his broad, flat face crackled vivid eagerness.

'It's gonna be a great night!' he greeted them with gusto. 'A great night!'

Seamus threw down an oyster, then wiped his mouth vigorously on his forearm and swung up to the ring. 'I'll see you ladies later—I'm corner man for the Boss.'

Butterfly gave his large bottom a slap. 'Don't let anyone cold deck him, Seamus!'

'Not a chance!' Seamus stepped through the ropes. 'The Boss'll flatten Dagget in three!'

Eden settled herself on the barrel. Gloved and veiled, her jacket buttoned to her throat, she was already beginning to feel the heat and her head was spinning from the pungent, mingled odours of sweating flesh, beer and fish and salt spray. She could feel the feverish excitement of the crowd around her, pulsing and beating like a giant heart.

Beside her, Butterfly blew a string of laconic smoke rings. 'Bet we seem like a pretty rough bunch to you,' the redhead mused.

'Well—' Eden hesitated. 'I'm afraid that at first you did. You see, until I came to the Golden Gate I'd never seen a world—people—like this.'

Butterfly snorted out a laugh. 'Didn't think you had, honey, but that's all right! The folks down here don't care where you been or where you're going—just as long as you play it straight with whatever hand you been dealt.' She winked at Eden. 'And, honey, you seem like a real straight player.'

Eden tingled with pleasure. It was the nicest compliment she'd ever received, perhaps the only real compliment she'd ever received. Freely given and from the heart, it had nothing to do with wealth or position.

Puffing contemplatively on her cigar, Butterfly hitched up one drooping satin shoulder strap and went on.

'Now me, I always knew there was a place like this somewhere—and I always knew I was gonna find it. You see, honey, I was born on a farm in Iowa—but I was dang sure I didn't want to die on a farm in Iowa!'

She grinned and crossed her legs.

'So, when I was sixteen, I headed West and ended up here. I knew right away this was the city for me. We've made it through the gold rush and the silver rush and the vigilantes—we used to burn down just about every other day! But each time we just grew up fatter and sassier than the time before! This is a city with a lot of spunk —just like me—and I ain't never leaving it!'

How wonderful to be so certain of your world! Of where and why you belonged! Eden Cortland had neither the luxury of a past or the promise of a future. But she had the moment.

Defiantly Eden tore off her hat and hurled it to the ground. She pulled off her gloves and unbuttoned her jacket, yanking if off. For one heady instant she felt as if she, too, belonged.

But all her fine feelings disappeared in a rush of jealousy as she saw Lily.

A hiss of catcalls and lewd remarks followed the blonde's progress through the crowd. Her spangled gown was deeply cut to expose her bosom and as she turned around to take a seat, she leaned over low to show even more of her melon-shaped breasts.

The rowdies clapped and stomped, calling for more yet, but even Lily was eclipsed by the deafening roar that went up as Chance Mallory stepped into the ring.

He was stripped to the waist, his hard-muscled body disciplined to a lean, hungry look, his face sharp and hard and clear. Turning, he came to his corner, standing with both hands spread wide on the ropes. Restlessly his eyes roamed the crowd—and then they fell on Eden.

She leaned forward and her body went taut. Beside her Butterfly was explaining the rules and regulations, the three minute rounds, the minute between, the ten-second count, but Eden was without hearing. Beyond her, Sykes Dagget was entering the ring, but Eden was without caring.

As on that first night, the world and all that was in it fell away. As on that first night, all her being—body and soul—was commanded by this unfathomable man who had come from the fog to change her life.

As once their glances had met and held across a Nob Hill banqueting room, so they did now—and in that moment it didn't matter that she knew too little of this man and even less of herself. Tonight she was one with Chance Mallory and he with her.

And as if in acknowledgement of this bond, he gave her a slight—ever so slight—nod of his head. Then he swung around.

The gong was sounded. The opponents stepped forward. The fight had begun.

From the first it was apparent that this would be a contest between brute strength and swift skill. Flat-footed, with his arms dangling nearly to his waist, his barrel chest matted with a black thatch as thick as any animal's, Dagget roamed the ring like some giant jungle creature. When his fists connected they fell like sledge hammers, but time and again, Chance delivered a spate of lefts and rights, then moved like lightning out of Dagget's range.

From the first it was also apparent that the Marquess of Queensberry's rules held little sway in any Barbary Coast bare-knuckle brawl. All kind and all manner of kicks, jabs, and wrestling holds were permitted—and encouraged by the hooting of the crowd.

It was near the end of the second round. With ape-like deftness, Dagget lunged forward, fists working like pistons. Chance countered, feinted, then delivered a long left to Dagget's mid-section that would have felled a lesser man. But Dagget merely grunted and shook it off, and bulled forward once more to catch Chance in the vice-like circle of his arms.

Chance's resistance threw Dagget off balance and together they plunged to the floor. Yet Dagget's brutal grip never loosened. Slowly, certainly, he was crushing out Chance Mallory's life.

Eden couldn't watch—but knew she must watch. Unaware of what she was doing, she grabbed Butterfly's hand between her own, digging in her nails with an intensity that drove a line of white half-moons into Butterfly's palm.

She couldn't watch—but she must watch. Watch

while Chance struggled for breath, biceps and stomach muscles knotted in agony.

Eyes shut with the effort, Chance brought up one knee, shoving it against Dagget's heavy belly, breaking his grip. Breathing like a wounded beast, Dagget stumbled upwards. As the gong sounded, he slumped back on to his stool.

Eden saw the murderous rage gleaming in his eyes. A rage not born of this night alone, but nurtured—developed—over several long-simmering weeks. His hands doubled into fists—fists, Eden knew now, that could kill.

No, Eden could not watch—but she must watch, through the third round, the fourth, the fifth.

A sneer on his swarthy, simian face, Dagget pursued his quarry across the ring, the great bole of his chest rising and falling. Countering right, then left, then jabbing his fists as if at a target, Chance fought with narrow-eyed concentration. With each round his lithe body seemed to grow stronger, surer. With every blow, the crowd roared its approval, screamed its rage, surging to its feet again and again in boisterous excitement.

But Eden saw nothing—thought of nothing—but the auburn-haired man in the ring. Like the beating of her own heart she felt the pulsing oneness between them—a current that ran so swift now, so strong, that not even Lily could break it.

The blonde burst from the crowd in a break between rounds. Displaying her ample rump to the audience, her front to Chance, she bent low through the ropes, grabbing up the sponge from Seamus to wipe Chance's face, his streaming shoulders.

With no regard for delicacy, Seamus booted her back-side out of the ring, and hands on her hips, she stood for a moment staring at Chance. Then deliberately she moved her gaze to Eden—and at the sly triumph on that painted face, Eden felt strange fingers of dread begin creeping towards her stomach.

Lily broke away and began running towards the street. Eden watched the blonde head bobbing and weaving through the crowd. The sound of the gong turned her eyes again to the ring—but it didn't dispel her fear. The dread persisted.

Persisted and grew as she saw Chance come slowly off his stool. As if to clear his brain he shook his head, then passed a hand over his eyes. His flagging steps were those of an old, tired man.

The fingers of Eden's fear became a clenched fist, squeezing her breath—her body—to nothingness. With round eyes of horror she watched Chance stagger across the ring, barely able to keep his fists up.

Seamus was screaming advice. The crowd was scream-ing encouragement—insults—anything. Nothing pene-trated.

Chance took a blow to the jaw. His head bobbed back. He almost fell. Now Dagget bored in, driving his fists with the slogging force of twin hammers.

Sensing the kill, the crowd was on its feet, and Eden, too, was standing, leaning hard against the ropes. She felt the blows beating at her own body. She felt Chance's agony tearing at her heart.

Chance staggered. This time he went down. And in the thud of his body Eden heard her words of the night before, 'I want to see Sykes Dagget give you the thrashing of your life!'

Eden choked away her tears—her anguish. 'Chance,' she cried out, and then again.

She knew he could not hear her, but she did not care. With all the intensity of her soul she went on calling his name.

And, almost as if he had heard her, his eyes opened. Eden leaned over the ropes, stretching out her arms as if to infuse him with her strength—as if by the sheer force of her will she could summon him back from the fog into which he'd disappeared. Again and again she repeated his name, and on her face and in her voice was the tenderness she'd hidden all these long weeks but which she could hide no longer.

Chance looked at her—clung to her eyes. Slowly he pushed up to one elbow. He grabbed at the ropes. On the referee's nine count, he hauled himself to his feet, his chest heaving with the effort, his body pouring sweat.

Head down, Dagget charged him like a bull, but calling on the unconscious reflexes of a magnificently tuned body, Chance dodged sideways. Summoning up the final tenets of his strength, he spun out with both fists, delivering a left to Dagget's belly, a right to his jaw.

Dagget wavered. His knees bent. His huge body teetered backward, forward, and then he crashed face down like a felled tree.

The Golden Gate had been saved.

So sudden was this twist of fortune, the crowd was stupidly silent. Then, as the referee lifted Chance's hand high in victory, they went wild with approval.

Half-dazed, Eden stood silent in the midst of their cheers. But the sight of Chance falling back against the ropes in exhausted triumph brought her suddenly to.

The crystalisation of what she had found that night

rose and swelled within—tearing at her, leaping at her with a physical force.

She wanted to hurl herself into the ring, throw herself against him—throw away all the old rules and regulations and cling to him.

Almost—almost she took a step. But the crowd was already closing in, shutting her out, shutting her away.

Someone handed Chance a bottle and he took a long, deep swallow, then he was hefted high on Seamus's shoulders, the two of them swept away on a human tide.

Eden sagged back on to the barrel. She was limp with exhaustion—drained almost beyond movement. Too much had happened tonight. She'd known too much joy, felt too much pain. But that which she wanted most to know still eluded her.

'Butterfly,' she said in the spent voice of utter weariness, 'tell me about Chance Mallory.'

Butterfly threw her a long look and her harsh-featured face softened with understanding, and sympathy. The redhead lit a cigar, waved out the match and tossed it into the water.

'Pride, honey,' she said at last, 'that's what Chance Mallory is all about. Pride in who he is and where he comes from. Pride—that's what keeps him living in that room! He doesn't want any part of rich folks' trappings. Pride's what makes him use his own dough to help the people down here—*his* people. He's always staking some poor sucker down on his luck to a free room and board and a new start. A coupla times he's even dug into his own pockets to pay the mortgage money on a joint ready to go under.'

'The poke due on the Silver Dollar,' Eden murmured, her mind going sharply back to the first words she had ever heard Chance Mallory utter.

Now she knew what they meant and why they had been spoken. Pride had brought Chance Mallory to Nob Hill that first night. Pride was what led Chance Mallory down all his days. Pride and that strange, simmering hatred.

The redhead frowned. 'What did you say, honey?'

Eden waved aside her question. 'It's nothing. Please —go on.'

Butterfly ducked her head towards a clump of dingy flats, so crowded, side by side and one on top of the other, it seemed impossible that the sun could ever penetrate.

'The Boss was born in a joint like that. Seems he never knew his father—or at least none of us have ever heard him talk about his father. 'Course that's how it is with the Boss, he don't answer any questions and he don't ask 'em. I guess that's the way it is with most of the folks down here.'

Pondering her own words, Butterfly took a thoughtful puff or two. The torches had been doused and as once again the moon slipped behind feathered clouds, the two women were wrapped in blackness. Only the sound of lapping water and the faraway echo of the crowd broke the night silence. And then Butterfly went on.

'I heard it from Seamus that Chance's mother worked as a barmaid—I guess the Boss and Seamus go a long ways back. Anyway, his ma got the consumption and Chance started kicking around the waterfront when he was just a little boy, doing whatever he could to bring home money. He did a turn on the docks, shined shoes, ran bets from one saloon to the other. I guess he even worked for a while as a stable boy at one of the big houses on Nob Hill. But he didn't much like that and came back here.'

'No,' Eden said softly, seeing the boy the man had sprung from, envisioning the bitterness that had grown day by day. 'I don't suppose he did like that.'

'Then when he got older there were other things—a little smuggling for the boys in Chinatown, a little gambling—though the Boss has always been too smart to do much of that. Some of his jobs landed him in a cell for a day or two—but he always came out ready for more. It was when he and Seamus were laying tracks for the cable cars—swinging ten-pound sledge hammers twelve hours a day—that he fought his first fight. The boys in his crew put him up against a Russian bruiser, a whaler. The Boss knocked the tar outta him in a round!'

Butterfly shook her red head in admiration.

'Anyway, the Boss kept on fighting—and winning. Seamus told me he wanted to earn enough money to get his mother outta the rat hole they were living in—get her a proper doctor. The night he won the Golden Gate he went home to tell her to pack up—and found the building had burnt to the ground. And his mother with it.'

Butterfly's words were matter-of-fact, but their very straightforwardness held a special horror. In the wake of that unflinching voice, Eden could say nothing. Mere words could not give voice to what she was thinking —feeling.

She had wanted to hear Chance Mallory's story, but the telling of it had brought her not peace but rather a dawning understanding. A dawning anger at her own world, and the people who lived so carelessly with their wealth.

Eden dropped her eyes to the water. As unfathomable as black glass it lay. Abruptly she picked up a loose piece of wood and threw it down. The water rippled and eddied—but it did not break. And neither, Eden knew, did the people who lived in those grey, dingy buildings, so far from the sunshine—and privilege. Neither did Chance Mallory.

Silently Eden stood. Silently she walked with Butterfly back to the Golden Gate.

CHAPTER
SEVEN

WITHOUT thought, without reason, Eden sought Chance Mallory.

With impatient eyes she searched the Golden Gate, scanning the gaming tables, the bar. With swift steps she mounted the stairs to the barren bedroom on the third floor.

Her hunger for this man had been fed by the current that had beat between them tonight—flamed by the new understanding Butterfly's words had created. Need had overcome reason—and she pressed on.

Quickly she travelled down the hall to the training room. And there her search ended.

Chance lay on a long narrow table, his head resting on folded arms, his eyes closed. Bending above him was Ah Wan, his wizened hands massaging Chance's naked back.

Eden felt her knees go weak, all sanity swept aside by her desire to hold her hand against his cheek, caress away the weariness of his body. An hour before, the crowd had taken him from her. But now there was no one to hold her away. Quietly, quickly she came into the room.

'Leave us, Ah Wan,' she said softly.

'Missy Boss!'

Ah Wan's raisin eyes popped and he launched into a spray of protesting whispers—no less vehement for their softness. 'No gel can come in here! Go away, Missy Boss! Go way! No gels in here!'

But Eden had learned how to handle him.

'Leave us, Ah Wan,' she repeated and when he opened his mouth to protest, she raised an eyebrow to counter him.

Ah Wan folded his lips one over the other. His little body puffing up like an affronted toad, he trotted from the room, muttering a string of what Eden had no doubt were Chinese epithets.

For only a moment Eden hesitated, then gently she placed her palms against Chance's shoulders and a violent shudder shook through her body. With slow, languorous strokes she began working her hands down his back.

His skin was warm beneath her touch and the hardness of his body—so near, too near—drew her closer still and she bent low, letting the loose tendrils of her black hair graze the hollow of his neck. As her breasts pressed into his back, she shivered with pleasure.

'Your touch is very different from Ah Wan's.'

Eden went rigid.

'You were awake,' she murmured and her voice was an agony of shyness. 'You knew I was here—'

'I've known all along.'

Eden's breath caught in her throat and as if he could see the wantonness in her eyes, feel the wanting in her touch, she jerked her gaze from his body—tore herself upright. Yet already she knew she had betrayed too much.

Her tenderness had not been for the telling—to reveal herself to the sleeping Chance Mallory was one thing, but to come as she had to a Chance Mallory in full possession of his senses was quite another. She turned to flee.

Sharply Chance came about and one hand shot out to close around her wrist.

'Let me go,' she begged with a mounting desperation.

'You can pull away if you like.'

Eden looked at her hand. Only lightly did it lie imprisoned in his. Once before she'd been given the choice and once before, with Chance Mallory's eyes on her, she'd hesitated. As she hesitated now.

With a surprising gentleness Chance drew her down against him. His face was blank, his eyes blazing with some unnameable fire.

'Go on,' he said quietly, 'finish the rub down.'

Eden bowed her head and the black arc of her lashes cast a slanting line over the curve of her cheek. From the lace collar her throat rose slender and white, the sweep of her profile as cool as marble, as clear as a cameo. Yet at the very touch of his body fire broke within her and she was lost.

Hesitantly, and then with a mounting desire she could not control, Eden ran her caress over his shoulders, through the burnished hair that matted his chest, down the contours of his torso. She felt his body twitch and tauten beneath her hands, she felt his following gaze like a steely flame.

The scent of him filled her nostrils, her longing for him drawing the last particle of sanity from her senses. Softly sighing, parting, her lips brushed his skin.

'Eden,' he said in a voice so low, so intense, she wondered if she had dreamt it. For a fleeting moment what might have been tenderness crossed his face.

'I was with you tonight, Chance,' she whispered, her

words moving quietly through the rustle of her breathing. 'I want you to know that.'

His eyes narrowed and darkened, the hawklike features went rigid with wariness. Beneath her hands his whole being was strung tight. As fine as an indrawn breath, the silence stretched between them.

And then the anger drained from his body. He closed his eyes. 'I know,' he answered her, and there was no need to say more.

From that first moment tonight their hearts had been as one—and, fight against it though he might, he could deny it no longer.

His tension gone, his face was shadowed with exhaustion and Eden felt her desire give way to a need to do something for him. Turning, she scooped out a handful of Ah Wan's white salve from its jade jar, gently rubbing it into the cuts above his eyes, across his cheekbones. Lightly—still shy—she smoothed the thick auburn hair from his brow, stroking the cooling ointment over his forehead.

She lifted one of his hands in hers, massaging it with salve, and seeing the bruises there she remembered how they had been inflicted—and why. With a caress that was an ache within, she pressed his hand to her cheek.

Deliberately Chance brought up his other hand, cupping them both against her face. 'I fought my way out of the slums with these hands,' he said softly.

'I know,' Eden's own voice was husky with a thousand suppressed emotions. 'Butterfly told me everything—about the fire—your mother—'

'So you know,' he echoed her, and his words came out flat and calm, their very emptiness stirring a fearful coldness in her heart.

'That's why I came here,' Eden faltered, driven by the compulsion to share her new-found understanding with him—yet held back by a strange instinctive fear. 'I came to let you know—to tell you—'

'To tell me what?' His eyes opened and they were as glass, boring holes through her soul. 'How sorry you were for me?'

'No!' Eden cried. 'That isn't it!'

'Isn't it?'

His face was without fury, his voice without rage, but there was in his quiet face, his still voice, that which burned too hot for mere anger. He moved his hands up and under her hair, tightening them against her temples until at her cry of pain, a small smile seared his lips. He released her and with the sharpness of a jack-knife recoiling, he came to his feet.

'You put on quite a show tonight, Miss Cortland, do you know that? Coming in here all full of compassion and duty—just like those ladies who used to visit the tenements once a week with their baskets of food.'

'No—' Eden whispered again. She pressed her hands to her lips, helplessly shaking her head against his words. She wanted to cry out that he had understood nothing, but she could not explain what she herself did not comprehend.

'Well, I'm not interested in your sympathy—or anything else you have to offer. Get out of here—leave me alone!'

Slowly Eden's head lifted.

'I will go,' she said clearly, and the effort needed to control her voice made it sound hard, 'and with pleasure. But first I want to tell you that I was wrong when I said I wasn't sorry for you. I *am* sorry for you, Mr

Mallory, sorry that you can't accept kindness when it is freely given, sorry that the shell you've built around yourself has made you no more than an animal, trapped in a cage of self-pity!'

Chance paled beneath his tan, his face twitching as though stung. Swiftly he spun around—Eden's last glimpse of him was of his rigid back as he stared through the window at the black night of the Barbary Coast.

Rain was falling across San Francisco. Driven by the wind it swept in foggy sheets down the hills, flooded the streets, lashed the windows. And that leaden rhythm of wind and rain was the dull, pounding pain of Eden's heart.

Chance had been gone from the Golden Gate for two weeks.

During that time not even Seamus had received word from him—or if he had, he'd said nothing to Eden. And she was too proud to ask. Head high she went about her business. With Butterfly's aid—for her red head harboured a shrewd brain—she laboured over the books. With the help from Seamus she had spurned before, she struggled to supervise the mad revelry of the gilded room.

In Chance's absence the total management of the Golden Gate had fallen to her—yet it was a hollow victory.

Never once did she mention Chance Mallory's name, but never was he out of her thoughts. For if Eden did not know where he was, she knew who he was with. Lily, too, had disappeared, and a hundred times a day the thought of that voluptuous body pressed to his drove a dagger through Eden's heart.

A hundred times a day, with galling bitterness, her mind fled back to the night of the fight—and her face crimsoned at the memory. A hundred times a day she cursed herself for that foolish offering of her compassion.

Yet if the days were bad, the nights were worse. For it was then that she dreamt. And now, night after night, it was a man who emerged from the mist of her dreams. A man with a hawklike face and steel blue eyes. A man who didn't want her.

Yes, during the waking hours she could keep desperately busy. It was at night, when she lay alone in the massive brass bed, that the real pain began.

Sometimes, when there was a rare afternoon of sunshine, Eden would seek respite from her thoughts. In pin-striped shirtwaist and a skirt shortened to her ankles, a straw boater on her coronet of braids, she would climb into a cable car with Seamus and Butterfly, with Ah Wan, picnic hamper in hand, wedged between them. Up the hills they'd climb, then plunge straight down, the passengers shouting warnings to one another as they swung around the corners almost at right angles.

At Ocean Beach everyone would pile out, the white sand brimming with picnickers and bathers. Clad in a daring knee-length swimming costume, saucy bloomers and black stockings, Butterfly would take to the water, while Seamus, whale-like in his red striped two-piece suit, lumbered happily after her.

Wandering along the shore, the salt spray thick on her lips, Eden would wave to them, then finally settle herself in the sand. Arms clasped around her drawn-up knees, hat off to let the wind whip through her hair, she would watch the breakers pound against the rocks and roll up towards her feet sending the sandpipers scurrying. When, blood-red, the sun dropped into the ocean, she would rise—and they would all start off for the Golden Gate again.

One day at the end of March, they'd journeyed to the beach only to be caught in a downpour on the way home. And that night the storm still pounded against darkened windows.

Wrapper-clad, Eden sat in her bedroom, listening to the mounting ferocity of rain and wind. Around and around in her hands she turned a cup of steaming tea.

'Velly bad! Velly bad!'

On small, slippered feet Ah Wan scurried from the dressing-room where he'd been drawing her a bath. Pausing before the window he placed splayed fingers against the pane. 'Velly bad,' he muttered again.

'What's very bad?' Eden asked absently. She stood and stretched, then took a sip of tea. 'The rain?'

Ah Wan came close and his lemon-tinged face, all wrinkled skin and bones, was suddenly sallow with fear.

'It's an omen, Missy Boss,' he whispered in a voice less jangling than she had ever heard him use. 'Omen! The animals know! Cats—dogs—birds—all leave! Bad things coming for this city! I go Chinatown—see it in the cards—bad things coming!'

In the room's dim light, with the rain sounding a menacing tattoo outside, there seemed an unearthliness to Ah Wan's words—a wisdom that went beyond this world. A link with forces unseen, unknown.

A crack of thunder cut the night. Eden started at the sound, the cup slipping from her hands to crash against the floor.

Stooping, Ah Wan began gathering up the pieces,

then he lifted his head and his black eyes shone like ebony beads.

'Take warning from Ah Wan, Missy Boss! Leave city now—go 'way—go East! Go home!'

Quickly Ah Wan ducked out through the door, leaving Eden staring, motionless, in his wake.

Home. Go home. But where was home?

She wondered if she'd ever known.

All this time—all these weeks—she'd been like Alice in *Through the Looking Glass*, running harder and harder to stay in one place. But she was not led by the Red Queen; she was carried by a man out of time and mind to a world she'd never known—and which yet held some unexplainable link to a past she could not fathom . . .

Sharply Eden turned. She went into the dressing-room and slid off her wrapper, and with a long sigh of release, slipped into the tub.

The water was pink-tinged from the bath salts, and rose-scented. Lying back, Eden let it foam and swirl about her breasts. There was a sensual pleasure in the steaming, fragrant touch of that water against her skin.

She shut her eyes. And now, as always, her thoughts turned to Chance Mallory.

She remembered every nuance of his face and body —the times she had touched him, the times she had not. This was exquisite torture . . . she should stop. But she could not—and her thoughts ran on.

She remembered Chance Mallory as he had been that night in the jail, fearless, a strong surety against the world. She remembered the animal-hard look of him in the ring, she remembered the feel of his chest beneath her hands.

She remembered him as she'd seen him that first night . . .

Like an echo from that night she heard the door crash open. Her eyes went wide. Framed against the wavering light she saw a man.

And now Eden knew she must be dreaming once more—for the man was Chance Mallory.

He was coatless, his white linen shirt stained with sweat and whiskey and hanging carelessly open. New lines cut deeply into the gauntness of his face and his jaw was shadowed by a stubble of beard. Like twin coals his eyes burned.

He kicked the door shut and came forward, and his voice was hoarse. 'I told you once before that a locked door couldn't keep me out.'

Wordlessly Eden looked up at him. She didn't know where he had been and she didn't care. She didn't know from whence he had come and it didn't matter. She only knew that, awake or dreaming, her need for this man tore at her with a physical pain—sweeping away everything in its path.

The steaming water had melted away the last, lingering remnants of her modesty—these last weeks of misery had erased all pride—and now the thick, hot quickening of desire was a fiercer torment than anything she'd known before.

She pressed flattened palms to the sides of her breasts and, holding his gaze, she ran her hands down her body.

She heard him catch a breath, saw his chest rise and fall, saw the gleam of sweat break out across his forehead—and she knew that his longing matched her own.

Electric moments passed, the current between them rising to the fever pitch of the storm outside.

'Eden—' he murmured, as he had once before, yet now his voice was taut and shaking with strain. 'Your skin was scented with roses that first night on Nob Hill, like it is now—'

Sharply he spun on his heel, towards the dresser, where a row of crystalline bottles stood. 'And did you bring these trinkets with you from Nob Hill—like you brought your silken clothes and your elegant manners—'

His voice broke. With one sudden thrust of his arm he swept the bottles to the floor and, as the sound of shattering glass crashed around them, he lifted her from the water and into his arms.

Savagely his mouth crushed hers—her own lips demanding more. Her hair cascaded loose from its pins to fall about them both like a veil, and she pressed her wet, scented body to his in a long, aching caress.

He carried her to the bed and laid her down and kissed her again, his bruising lips scalding her throat, her shoulders. But his very violence was freeing a sensuality she'd never known she possessed and she answered him kiss for kiss, frenziedly moving her hands against his naked chest, his hard muscled thighs.

On straightened forearms, Chance leaned over her. His chiselled face was savage with desire, his nostrils flared. Slowly, deliberately, he buried his lips against her softly curving breasts.

A low moan caught in Eden's throat, her body writhing in an agony of delight as his hands swept over the slender moulding of her hips, across her thighs.

'Please,' she whispered, 'oh, please—' Her eyes closed with the intensity of her passion. 'Please take me—' she moaned—and her surrender was complete.

Slowly Chance drew away. Her body throbbing with unanswered need, Eden reached out blindly for him. Her eyes opened—and his face rose up before her, mocking and triumphant.

'Tell me, Miss Cortland,' he asked with studied cruelty, 'how does it feel to beg?'

Eden drew in a harsh breath. She jerked her hand from him, bringing it against her lips—and not until later did she discover she'd set her teeth into the skin, drawing blood.

'The rich are used to getting what they want, aren't they?' he went on in that cool, brutal voice. 'Well, this is one night when you had a taste of what it's like to be poor.'

A sob choked in Eden's throat, but she could not summon the strength for tears. As if the preceding moments had wiped away all dignity—as if she were crushed beyond caring—she made no effort to hide her nakedness. She just lay there, and the black eyes that rested on him were stripped bare with pain.

From the moment Chance Mallory had bolted into her life from the fog, he'd wanted to see her beaten before him—defenceless. And now he'd obtained his wish.

'You've done what you set out to do,' she said in a voice that pulsed with her own sick shame. 'You've humiliated me. Now please go.'

Chance lunged forward and seized her arm in a wrenching grip, pulling her up.

'Fire and ice,' he said savagely, and there was a dark, nameless hurt glittering from behind the steel of his eyes, 'that's what you are! All finishing school manners on the surface—but underneath you're no different from any of the waterfront strumpets.'

Her jerked her close, his face burning only inches from hers. 'Well, the next time you pretend to be so ladylike—so clean and pure—remember tonight.'

Contemptuously he flung her away. Eden covered her face with shaking hands at the beat of his hard strides across the floor. The door slammed, her body jerking convulsively at the sound.

As if she were moving through water, she lifted down her hands. She felt her body through a haze of pain . . . she felt soiled to her soul. And shamed, desperately shamed.

How easily she'd walked into Chance Mallory's trap! Well, he'd been right and she'd been wrong. The Barbary Coast was no place for her. She was too vulnerable . . . her soul too raw for the life here. The past moments had proved that.

Now she wanted only to rip the heart from her body and never feel again—now she wanted to retreat to the hollow peace of her past, to move again among men and women who didn't love or hate—or hurt.

From the ashes of her torment had come one bittersweet comfort—and one clear thought. At last she knew where she belonged.

Tomorrow she would leave the Golden Gate and the Barbary Coast forever.

CHAPTER
EIGHT

THE Palace Hotel was the most fashionable eating place in San Francisco.

Its centre court, surrounded by columned galleries six storeys high, was crowded with potted palms and stone statues and dancing fountains, its vaulted, glassed-in ceiling reflecting gleaming silver, cut glass bowls, shining white napery. The air was filled with expensive perfume and fresh flowers, and champagne flowed like water into crystal goblets.

And at the Palace Hotel, the pre-theatre hour was the most fashionable time of the day. Everywhere were men and women who came not so much to share an early supper as to be seen. And among them were Eden Cortland and her guardian.

As if he had been welcoming her home from no more than a morning's shopping spree, so had Julius greeted Eden on her return to Paxton Place. Lenore she never saw.

Only at night would Eden hear those restive footsteps pacing the floor, ever pacing. But when she knocked on the door there was no answer. When she tried the knob she found it locked. Like someone long dead, Lenore Paxton was never seen. And never mentioned. Nor was the Golden Gate—or Eden's reasons for fleeing there.

Once more, and as if without a pause, Julius had

picked up the golden threads of her life. Once again he began to wind them about her.

He'd taken her everywhere in these two weeks since her return, to small parties, to grand balls, to the theatre, to the opera. The dresses she had arrived with and worn during her days on the Barbary Coast, he'd ordered given away. In their stead he had purchased a whole new wardrobe for her, frothy tea gowns and silken reception suits, evening dresses with drop shoulders and négligés of Valenciennes lace, tulled hats and hand-painted parasols, and satin slippers seeded with pearls —and all in white. Always in white.

The dress Eden wore this evening had been Julius' gift. Austerely plain, it fell in the unbroken Gibson Girl sweep from *décolletage* to hem, the severity of its style only accenting the slender lines of her body.

Save for the single, flawless diamond Julius had hung about her throat that afternoon, her arms and neck were bare of jewellery, their creamy whiteness a rare kind of adornment, her only other accessories the white tuber-oses pinned to the raven's wing coils of her hair. Start-lingly black, her slanted eyebrows swept up against her ivory skin, and beneath them her gaze smouldered darker than her hair.

Like some exquisitely cultivated flower, Eden sat in this hothouse of fashion. But the expression on her face was one of strain. She looked wary, guarded—as if haunted by some thought against which she must keep constant vigil.

And so she must.

Since the night she'd left the Golden Gate, she'd had to fight against a threatening torment of memories. They must never break their bonds—not ever. For if they did,

she would be helpless before them. Helpless—and forever lost.

'You're finished?' Julius asked solicitously.

Eden nodded, pushing away her untouched dessert.
'Thank you, Julius. It was a delicious meal.'

'Then I propose a toast.' He lifted his glass high and
his voice was a ringing bell. 'To the deed you signed
yesterday—to my new controlling interest in the Golden
Gate!'

Eden flinched. A tiny pin-prick of warning pierced her
heart. Desperately she clenched all that was within her
tight against the impending pain.

But in almost hypnotised fascination, she stared at
Julius' hands as they held his goblet. Hands as slender
and white as a woman's—a world away from the hard,
calloused hands of a man who had used his fists to fight
his way out of the slums—

Eden took a swift breath, gripping the stem of her own
goblet so hard her hand shook.

Julius' thin brows lifted to crescents. 'You do not
drink, Eden?'

'I—I'm sorry—'

She forced a sip of the ruby wine past her lips, but the
taste was gall.

'Perhaps you wish you hadn't signed the deed,' Julius
pursued. He paused and tilted his well-shaped head
sideways and his eyes—hidden as always behind the
thick lenses of his spectacles—watched her. 'Perhaps
you long to return to the Golden Gate—and Chance
Mallory.'

The floodgates burst wide—the onslaught of Eden's
pain was a suffocating thing. She dropped her goblet, the
wine spilling thickly over the damask cloth.

'How clumsy of you, my dear,' Julius' soft tones were at disturbing variance with the sudden harsh lines of his face. He looked down at the spreading stain and as if mesmerised, kept staring.

'How rich the wine is, how red . . . like fire . . .'

Like some sleeping beast roused to life, that old, remembered premonition of doom began stirring again in Eden's breast. Unaware of what she was doing, she came to her feet and the droplets of wine clung crimson to her white gown.

Immediately she was engulfed by a bewildering array of waiters, all bowing and scraping, all wiping at her dress. All apologising, for what she didn't know.

Again, with that near deadly fascination, Eden looked at her guardian, watching him as he accepted her cape from the maitre d', his silk top hat, his gold-headed walking stick, his pearl-buttoned gloves.

As if she, too, were one of his possessions, Julius took her hand, drawing it through the crook of his arm. As she had once before, Eden recoiled from his touch—but this time Julius did not let it pass.

'Why do you pull away?' he asked pleasantly, the odour of sandalwood rising up from his pores like a whisper. 'Surely you don't mean to run away from me again?'

With a spidery strength surprising in one so small, Julius tightened his grip on her arm and led her through the hotel. Once outside he dismissed the coachman, helping her himself into the carriage.

'I have a special surprise for you tonight, Eden—and I don't want to be bothered with servants' prying eyes.' He laughed lightly. 'Ah, yes, I have a very special surprise for you!'

The late afternoon fog was drifting in from the harbour, curious tendrils of mist floating through the streets, seeping down the hills, hovering around the buildings.

Within the sheltering calash, the gauzy hood of her cape as white as winter snow against her black hair, Eden sat like a wraith sprung herself from the mist. Beside her Julius was silent—and that silence was an overpowering thing, building about them as the fog built. And with it built Eden's foreboding. For the first time in weeks something mattered, but it mattered with a dread that had begun her pulse beating in fear.

Eden wanted to leap from the carriage and run, up the hills, away—but away from what and to where? Her locked heart would not permit her to return to the Golden Gate. And there was nowhere else—nowhere else on earth—to go.

Through the thickening fog, Julius drove on, coming to a section so densely packed he had to slow the carriage to a snail's pace. The streets here held an exotic look and Eden realised they were in Chinatown.

The air was awash with the smell of the fish markets and the almond scent of the opium dens. Beside the gilded pagodas, beneath cherry-red lanterns, passed a parade of colourful humanity, little men in purple brocaded coats and puffed silk trousers, coolies in coarse cotton with hats like inverted bamboo trays, doll-like women with sleek black heads and bound feet, leaning helplessly on their attendants' shoulders. There were other women, too, painted and brazen, hanging carelessly out of their bamboo brothels to beckon the men in.

The streets rang with the vendors' cries, desperate for

the last sale of the afternoon. Poles slung over their shoulders, produce overflowing from the baskets that dangled at either end, the vegetable and fruit pedlars haggled with knots of shouting housewives, while the purveyors of ivory and jade and silk knelt beside small teakwood tables and hawked their wares on the street corners.

'Eight dolla!' they cried, holding out bolts of material at elbow's length or delicate lacquered boxes in upraised palms. 'You like? All lite. Fi dolla!'

Rising, swirling, never ceasing, the eye-aching, ear-splitting panorama of colour and noise swept around the Paxton carriage. And all the time, as the mist deepened and the shadows fell, Eden's suspicion built within her, growing larger and larger until it threatened to smother her.

Julius drew rein before what was no more than a dismal shack. As if he were escorting her to afternoon tea, he ushered Eden from the carriage and through the narrow door.

Inside, the rank odour of cheap liquor and sweat was stomach turning, the floor filthy with damp sawdust, the ceiling smoke-stained. All around were rude benches and tables, and peering through the murky air, Eden saw almond-eyed maidens plying the sailors who sat there with liquor.

The girls were young, but their ebony eyes were old, and etched on their faces was a glazed numbness as deep as the slack-jawed drunkenness of the sailors.

No one looked up at the two new entrants.

'Come, Eden. We must proceed.'

At the thought of passing through the hell of that room, Eden's body stiffened in revulsion, but once again came that spidery pressure on her arm. Yet it was not the strength of Julius' body that held her in thrall, but the twist of excitement on that smooth face, the beating up of intensity in that courtly voice—the strange something that lay hidden behind the heavy spectacles.

He led her through the smoky depths and down a dank hallway, and from behind curtained thresholds rose up the grunts and moans of animal-like ecstasy. They paused before a heavy door, Julius pushing it open with his walking stick. Like the ladder to hell, rickety stairs rose up from a subterranean cavern.

'Your surprise awaits you below, my dear.'

Eden stared into the blackness, Julius' words starting a chill down her spine. Then, gathering up her skirt in one hand, she descended. The air below was cool and musty, the walls hung with lanterns, and lounging like snakes at the bottom of a pit, bottles in their hands, were men Eden knew. Dagget's men.

Now Eden's premonition was a premonition no longer, but stark fear. She could not fathom it, could not understand it any more than she could understand any part of this terrible night, yet it was as real as her next breath—a living thing gnawing at her insides.

She turned to run—but her steps brought her hard against Sykes Dagget. His simian face was contorted into a sneer and behind him, Julius was smiling too.

'Captain Dagget is in my employ,' Julius said amiably. 'Indeed, it's the Captain and his men we have to thank for—catching—your surprise. Captain—' he nodded towards a door built into the earthen wall. 'Would you be so kind as to show my ward her surprise.'

'With pleasure, Mr Paxton!'

Dagget's heavy hand shot out to open a small slot in

the door. With mock gallantry, he motioned Eden towards it.

She made no move.

'Please,' Julius urged, as if offering her a glimpse of some fine statue or painting. His voice sharpened. 'I insist.'

Slowly Eden walked to the door and looked through the slot. In a corner of what was no more than a filthy hole, his back to the wall, his knees drawn up, was Chance Mallory.

His face was haggard, his eyes closed. Running the length of one cheek and matted with dried blood was a deep welt, a purple bruise at his temple. Yet his head was erect—as Eden knew it would always be.

She pressed her forehead against the door and shut her eyes. 'Why—' she whispered and could say no more.

'Why is he here?' Julius finished for her politely. 'He's been shanghaied—a common enough practice on the Barbary Coast when a Captain needs a crew.'

'Shanghaied,' Eden echoed in a broken voice that yet grew stronger with every angry word. 'You mean he was beaten senseless—and now Dagget and his men will drag him aboard their ship to serve against his will!'

'Exactly.'

With measured strokes, Julius smoothed down gloves that already fit like a second skin, and his silken voice was a flood of eloquence.

'There's a clause in the deed you so recently signed, my dear ward, to the effect that should the managing partner of the Golden Gate be away from the premises for more than six months at any one time, he automatically forfeits his share. Captain,' Julius asked carelessly, 'where are you bound for this voyage?'

'The regular run,' Sykes Dagget ran both hands over oily black hair. 'China!'

'China,' Julius repeated amiably. 'Well, then, Mr Mallory shall certainly be gone for a year at least—which means the Golden Gate becomes mine alone.'

Still intent on his gloves, Julius went on.

'You see, Eden, I brought you to San Francisco for the express purpose of gaining control of your Barbary Coast saloon. I thought it would be a simple matter to persuade you to sign over your share of an edifice you knew nothing about! But my plans were tampered with. How angry I was that night you returned to Paxton Place from the Golden Gate—your guilty secret blazing in your eyes! And when you fled the next morning—'

Julius paused and looked up, and on his face Eden saw something more dreadful than rage.

'I tried so many ways to wrest the Golden Gate from you, Eden! But for such a docile-seeming young woman you were most stubborn. I ordered Dagget and his men to insult you—to start that brawl—I hoped that would frighten you into leaving. When you so conveniently offered yourself up for jail I thought surely an encounter with Officer Cross would send you scurrying back to Nob Hill—he's one of the most effective men in my employ.'

'Sergeant Cross,' Eden repeated in fascinated horror. 'He's one of your creatures—'

'As are a hundred others—as is Lily. I must admit her idea of the drugged sponge between rounds was a brilliant one—the entire fight seemed a godsent opportunity! Had Lily—and Captain Dagget—prevailed, the Golden Gate would have fallen easily into my lap. But alas, they failed. And then—' he paused, and though his voice was quiet, there was that in it which started Eden

trembling, 'when I thought all was lost, you appeared
—willing—even eager!— to oblige me!'

Julius pivoted.

'Captain Dagget, what would you say Chance Mallory's life will be like aboard your ship?'

'Living hell,' Dagget answered with swift brutish anticipation.

'Living hell,' Julius repeated softly, slowly, revelling in the sound. 'Ah, yes, that will be most suitable!' Two hectic patches of colour appeared on his pale cheeks. 'I could easily have had Chance Mallory killed—but this is better. Far better! The Golden Gate will be lost to him and aboard Captain Dagget's ship he will know a torture more subtle than death. Ah, yes! This is far, far better!'

'Why—why do you want him to suffer so?' Eden managed, the horror of Julius' words constricting her throat.

'Because I hate him,' Julius replied and there was a world of meaning in that brief reply. 'I hate him more than the devil himself.'

Julius came forward. Dispassionately he looked through the narrow slot. 'Chance Mallory and I go a long way back, my dear Eden. I've waited forever to see him like this—to think of him suffering a fate far worse than death.'

'No!' Eden whispered, backing up a few frantic steps. 'No! I won't allow Dagget to take him! I'll go somewhere —tell someone—the police—'

'Officer Cross, perhaps?' Julius cut in with vicious irony. He shot out a sudden hand to seize Eden's face in his spidery grip, crushing her cheeks against her teeth, and his voice rose to an almost musical pitch. 'Just try to escape—just try! At my command any one of these fine fellows would break you in two as if you were no more than a piece of flotsam.'

Julius released his grip merely to stroke one finger across her tingling cheek. Violently Eden twisted away from his touch, bracing her back against the wall, searching his face for some sign of humanity—but there was none.

Julius laughed softly.

'Now tell me, my dear, for I've been longing to know, just what did Chance Mallory do to you that sent you running back to Paxton Place—that leaves you shaken at the mention of his name—pale at the sight of him?'

Abruptly Julius lashed his walking stick against the wall. 'Tell me!'

Eden pushed herself upright. Desperate hope was flooding the blackness of her mind—puncturing the dark dread clinging to her senses. With tingling coldness she hatched a plan.

'He taught me to beg,' she said clearly. 'As I'm begging you now—for five minutes alone with him.'

'Five minutes.'

Consideringly Julius tapped the gold-headed cane against the floor. 'All right,' he said finally, 'but five minutes and no more—the stench in here is insupportable.'

Julius nodded to Dagget, who shot back the bolt—but as Eden started, head high, through the door, Julius touched her arm with his cane.

'Remember, I'm allowing this solely for the amusement of watching your farewell—and watch I will. Every moment—every move.'

Eden nodded her understanding. Behind her, she heard Dagget bolt the door again. Determinedly she walked forward. A single swinging lantern hung from the ceiling and before the dim shadows that held Chance Mallory, she stopped.

'Chance—' Her voice was no more than a scented breath.

Slowly he looked up, and as he did, Eden fell to her knees before him, a flood of aching warmth releasing the congealed blood in her veins.

She knew now that the foreboding that had gripped her had been fear for this man—the link between them was forged of steel and could not be broken. His pain was hers. With all the tenderness of her shaking body, she cupped her hands about his bruised face.

For a moment naked emotion blazed in Chance's eyes. Across his face passed disbelief, joy—and something more. As if to assure himself that she was real, his hands came over hers.

Then his eyes narrowed, a look of fury twisting his falcon features. Savagely he flung her away and came to his feet, holding himself away from her as if she were poison.

'Haven't you had enough slumming, Miss Cortland? Or did you come here to gloat? Yes, that must be it—you couldn't resist the opportunity to parade your victory.'

Helplessly Eden shook her head, standing again. 'I—I don't know what you mean—'

'The hell you don't!'

His mouth creased into a bitter grin, his voice harsh and strained. 'It was your note telling me you needed my help that brought me here. Well—you've seen what you came for. Get out.'

'I sent no note,' Eden whispered with passionate

intensity. 'You must believe me! Julius must have used that as a ploy to get you here—' Her black eyes leaped. 'I want only to help you!'

Chance turned his head to that old wary angle, looking at her from beneath lowered lids. 'And if I don't want your help?'

Slim and fragile as a candle flame, Eden stood before Chance Mallory, yet against the tumbled black hair, her face held a desperate strength.

'As a Barbary Coast kidnapper once said to a lady,' she said evenly, 'you're in no position to tell me anything right now.'

Chance laughed on a terse note and a corner of his hard mouth shot upwards. 'Nicely put, Miss Cortland.'

Eden stepped close.

'We haven't much time—and Julius is watching our every move. We must pretend—pretend to embrace—' She drew a steadying breath. 'Put your arms around me.'

'You're getting more like a Barbary Coast wench daily,' Chance murmured in a low, gibing tone, but Eden did not care. As if of their own volition, her arms wound about his neck.

'Put your arms around me!'

And now Chance moved abruptly to her command, crushing her so hard against him she could feel his iron-hard chest through the flimsy stuff of her gown. Her head fell back, her parted lips inches from his. On his face she saw written a tormented struggle—felt his arms shaking as if to hold himself rigid against her. And leaping in her own body was a terrible joy that went past sanity—that warred with all reason.

'The gun you gave me,' she murmured through the rustle of his hard breathing, 'it's near my heart—'

And so it had been since the day she'd left the Golden Gate. For the touch of it against her skin—cold, hard, dangerous—had been his touch. For all these long weeks it had been the only link with him she'd permitted herself.

A muscle clenched in his heavy jaw. Eyes fixed on hers, Chance set his hand against her throat, then let it move to her bodice and below. Tensely, his fingers curled around the tiny derringer.

'Now kiss me,' Eden whispered, her body swaying with a desire that even here—even now—she could not suppress.

Chance's breath left his lungs in an agonised explosion, then he bent his head and his mouth moved against hers with a fury that broke her lips against his teeth.

A low roaring, like the sound of the sea, pounded in Eden's ears and she felt their bodies fuse and become one. The thudding of his heart was hers—his hunger was her own.

Forgetful of this place, this time, she clung to him. Only when he tore himself fiercely away, did she remember this might be but a farewell.

Whatever happens to me!' he said in a voice hoarse with intensity, 'save yourself—'

A flood of new light spilled into the room, showing Sykes Dagget in heavy relief against the open threshold. Swinging his ape-like arms, he stalked forward, stopping before them to run a hand down his drooping moustache.

'Your time's up, little lady!' His eyes gleamed with brutal anticipation as he turned to Chance. 'And so's yours, Mallory—let's go!'

But as Dagget reached out a hand to seize his arm,

Chance shoved him away and drove the gun into Dagget's back.

'Don't make a sound,' Chance muttered as Dagget's jaw dropped in shock. 'I want you to get Miss Cortland out of here and away from Paxton, do you understand?'

'I—I can't,' Dagget whimpered, fear darkening his swarthy face. 'I can't do anything against Mr Paxton —he'll kill me.'

'If you don't,' Chance said deliberately, grinding the gun deeper, 'I'll kill you first. Now call your men.'

Nervously Dagget ran his tongue over his thick lips. When his voice came out, it was a bull-throated roar.

'Jack—Pete—'

But it was not Dagget's sailors who answered the summons. Rather, a small, slim shadow fell across their path.

CHAPTER
NINE

IN HIS silk hat and black broadcloth coat, his folded
hands resting lightly on the gold-knobbed walking stick,
Julius Paxton stood resplendent in respectability. But as
he slowly removed his spectacles to stare at Chance,
Eden saw what had been hidden there for so long.

It was the light of madness that raged in his brilliant
eyes.

'How delightful to see you again, Mr Mallory, holding
sway in this filthy hole like the King Rat.'

Chance's lips drew into a tight line over his teeth. 'In a
sewer, a rat's the thing to be.'

Julius laughed lightly. 'Quite so.'

Looking from one to the other, Eden was again
conscious of the driving current that pulsed between the
two men. A shackle of bitterness that bound them like
blood in an old, secret hatred.

Julius replaced his spectacles.

'From careful observation, I know that my ward has
somehow contrived to slip a weapon to you, Mr Mallory,
and I know that currently you have it pressed to Captain
Dagget's back. A knife is it? Or a small revolver? No
matter. You will be able to kill no more than one of
us—Sykes Dagget it seems is the likely choice at the
moment—and then you and Miss Cortland will again be
at my mercy.'

Julius strolled forward, swinging his cane as he came.

'Perhaps you would care to hear what I have in mind for Eden after your departure on Dagget's ship. The incident tonight, I'm afraid, has forced me to change my plans somewhat—but I can assure you, the end result will be most interesting.'

Through mounting waves of horror, Eden heard the silken voice. Instinctively she turned to Chance—seeking strength, hope.

'You will not look at him!'

A spasm of rage convulsed Julius' voice. He shot out his cane to Eden's face, turning her head towards him. 'You will look only at me—and you will listen! Ah, yes—you will listen!'

Ever so slightly, Julius increased the pressure of the gold knob against the sweep of Eden's cheek.

'Until tonight I had such a wonderful future planned for you, Eden. You were to be my wife. My consort! You seemed the perfect woman to me when you first arrived—well-bred, docile. How I adored showering you with gifts! Even after your escapade on the Barbary Coast, I was willing to forgive—forget. Oh, yes, I tried to forget! I burned all your clothes and dressed you like a virgin. But tonight—tonight I discovered your true character.'

Julius' voice rose ever higher, grew ever more rapid, the light of madness playing over his perfect features to distort his face to no more than a craven image of that other Julius Paxton.

'Lily was the one who started my suspicions—she watched you all the while you were at the Golden Gate, Eden—it was her hatred of you that brought her into my employ! She told me how it was with you and Mallory —and tonight, when you spilled the wine at the very mention of his name, I knew she'd been right! I knew I had to discover how deep his seal was set upon you! So I brought you here—to test you. And you failed my test! You threw yourself at him like a harlot—like a common slut—'

Julius' voice cracked. He drew a rasping breath, his face damp with sweat. For a space there was silence, then softly, insidiously, he began again and now his voice was no voice at all, but a whisper of evil, weaving a web of horror around them all.

'I have many interests on the Barbary Coast—in Chinatown. But my most profitable is the peddling of female flesh. Captain Dagget imports the girls from China, and on their arrival the wheat is sorted from the chaff. The lesser ones are brought here, to service the sailors, but a few—the rare ones—are taken to a special house of delight. And what could be rarer than a gently-raised, white petalled American flower?'

So saying, Julius let his cane travel the slim outlines of Eden's body like the devil's caress. 'Until you rot from disease, my dear Eden, you will spend the rest of your days as a Chinatown harlot—'

'You damn monster!' Chance spat out between clenched teeth. 'You'll never take her to your filthy brothel!'

Swivelling, Chance aimed the gun at Julius, but in his rage he had forgotten Sykes Dagget. The burly giant hefted an elbow against Chance's arm, sending his single shot smashing harmlessly into the ground.

Chance threw down the gun and lunged for Julius, as if to throttle him barehanded, but with vicious swiftness Julius brought down his cane against Chance's skull, knocking him to his knees.

As Eden's screams rang out, he delivered a second,

more telling blow, this time stretching Chance senseless on the ground. With a piteous cry, Eden cast herself to her knees beside him.

'How careless of you, Chance,' Julius said softly, staring downward with an odd glitter to his still face. 'I had expected better.' He lifted his head, motioning to Dagget. 'Take him.'

'No!' Eden screamed, casting herself over Chance's body as Dagget bent to do Julius' bidding. 'No!'

Impatiently Dagget flung her aside. But as he slung Chance over one shoulder, Eden came at him with all the fury of an aroused tigress. She raked her nails across his face, she beat at his body with her small fists.

Growling out an oath, Dagget delivered her a stinging blow that sent her to her knees.

Sobbing, arms outflung, Eden watched Dagget carry Chance out—and the sight seemed to break the last remnants of her strength. Her hands fell. Slowly she turned her gaze to Julius.

Deliberately he came forward. With practised deftness he removed a small phial from his pocket and twisted off the glass stopper, shaking the contents over his handkerchief. Smiling he looked down at Eden.

'This won't harm you, my dear,' he said softly, and his voice held the soothing sound of the devil's lullabye. 'It's only the tincture of poppy, casting its spell.'

Julius took up a handful of the black hair to yank back her head. Still smiling, he held the handkerchief poised for a moment above her ashen face. Then slowly he lowered it . . .

Through clouds of incense, Eden saw hazy figures pass before her eyes.

Almond-eyed the women were, clad in silk, and their touch on her skin was cool and soft as they slipped off her clothes . . . as they bathed her flesh in steaming, scented water . . . as they anointed her flesh with fragrant oil. Gossamer light their hands were as they draped a scarlet kimono over her shoulders.

Eden offered them no resistance. She could not. Her body was as limp as a rag doll's. Her mind . . . her mind was dull, misted, as if from strong drink.

Only once could she summon the strength to speak and then the name was torn from a pain so deep not even Julius Paxton's drugs could blur it.

'Chance . . .'

Leaning against two of the women, Eden was taken like a clumsy, stumbling child down a hallway and into a bamboo room. In the very centre of this room rose a silken dais. To this Eden was led.

The attendants eased her to her knees. Carefully they arranged the folds of her kimono, the waves of her hair. Then they left her. Alone Eden looked with clouded eyes across her bamboo cage.

The walls were hung with red silk and golden draperies, ivory figurines and jade vases were set in carved niches. On low teakwood tables sat porcelain bottles and small, delicate cups, and there was incense here, too, jasmine-scented, billowing up from ebony bowls. Fragile as a blossom, a young girl sat in one corner, strumming a lute with long, thin fingers.

Ringing the dais were soft cushions of crimson and azure, on which white men lolled. And beside them, Julius Paxton's hand-picked harlots. Uniformly slim and shapely, their exquisite faces were dusted with rice powder, their silken kimonos encrusted with gold, their black hair skewered with ivory combs. But their hollow eyes were the eyes of women old before their time. They were the eyes of the young girls in that other crude brothel.

Stark memory cut into Eden's shadowed mind. She felt a rush of old pity—new fear, both of them bringing the gradual return of her senses.

With dawning realisation, Eden looked at the men who lounged on the silken pillows. Men who wore the dress of businessmen and bankers and Nob Hill gentry, but who had been transported beyond the everyday by potent rice wine and the ministrations of beautiful slaves to a world where the delights of the flesh were their only thought.

And tonight Eden Cortland would join the ranks of those women, bought and sold to bring them that pleasure.

Like a trapped animal, Eden pushed slowly to her feet. The slitted sides of the kimono gave a sudden glimpse of slender legs and thighs, against the unrelieved scarlet silk her skin was chalk white, her hair falling in waves of liquid ebony to her waist.

Inflamed by this new sight, the men leaned forward with relish. Sweating, their eyes gleaming, they stared at her.

But Eden would let herself feel no shame. Her body they might degrade—but the core of Eden Cortland they could not touch. For that was sailing away on a ship of hell, bound on a voyage of death.

Chance was gone from her, but his memory was hers forever and from it rose an unquenchable strength. Measure for measure, Eden returned their stares. Head high, she faced them fearlessly.

The scent of sandalwood, heavier than all the other perfumes, snaked into the room. Like the stench of brimstone it filled Eden's nostrils, for she knew whose coming it portended. Slowly, sipping on a goblet of fruited liqueur, Julius Paxton entered the bamboo room.

Eden felt her flesh crawl with revulsion. Clenching her body against the bile rising within, she watched him come towards her.

Before the dais, Julius stopped. He thrust up a spidery arm towards the girl who stood there.

'Is she not a rare treat, gentlemen? Notice the un-blemished skin—the lustre of her hair—the graceful lines of her body! Quality, gentlemen—quality!'

In one fluid motion, Julius stepped up beside Eden. Smiling in the face of her disdain, he took her chin in his hands.

'Yes, a rare treat indeed! A scarlet flower plucked from the very steps of Nob Hill!' He turned her head towards him, murmuring softly, 'Yes, my dear Eden, a scarlet flower—for scarlet is the colour of your shame.'

Coolly Eden returned his glance. Coolly she studied him, and in her eyes was the loathing of one who looks through bars at some bestial creature. With deliberate contempt, she spat into Julius Paxton's face.

His hand dropped. His skin mottled, turning red, then purple. As if choking, he clutched at his collar, an inhuman sound breaking from his lips.

'You'll pay for that, my dear Eden—you'll pay dearly!'

Julius swooped to the front of the dais and his voice rose full-throated. 'Her flesh is for sale, gentlemen! She goes to the highest bidder!'

'I'll make the first bid.' From the open doorway

Chance Mallory's words cracked like a whip. He levelled a gun high. 'And I'll do it with this.'

In one flashing instant, Eden went from death to life. Across the flare of the flaming torches, she stretched out her arms—and the cry she uttered held a joy that was almost pain.

The goblet broke in Julius' grip. Unnoticed, blood spurted from his hand and dripped to the floor as he stared at Chance.

Then through the heavy silence came the noise of uproar, of tramping feet—shouting voices.

'Your men, Mr Mallory?' Julius asked in quiet, shaking anger. He pressed his hand to his chest, bloodstains spreading darkly across the black broadcloth. 'Would I presume too much to ask how you escaped from Captain Dagget?'

Chance smiled. The lean lines of his chiselled face were set and taut, his steely eyes holding the bite of a bullet.

'Lily. Your thugs failed, Paxton—she didn't die. At least not until after she staggered into the Golden Gate and spilled everything. My friends came to Dagget's ship—and at knife-point he told me where you'd taken Eden.' Chance's jaw set. 'And now *I'm* taking her.'

Without shifting his gaze or the gun from Julius, Chance extended an arm to Eden. Deliberately he started towards her.

Her own eyes fixed on the strong face like a life-line, Eden came forward on legs still unsteady. But with a swiftness that stopped her breath, Julius caught her arm. He seized one of the torches and the rage of its flame matched the scarlet-clad sweep of Eden's body.

'One more step, Mallory,' Julius said softly, 'and I'll burn the skin off her body.'

Chance halted, his body rigid with a fury barely held in check. 'Let her go,' he said through clenched teeth. He cocked the pistol. 'Let her go or I'll kill you where you stand.'

'Kill me if you like Mallory—but I'll see Eden in flames first!'

As if reflecting the madness boiling within, the fire's light danced and swirled over Julius' face. He moved the torch nearer to Eden—so near she could smell the searing heat singeing her hair, hear its crackling.

Head still high, she was trembling all over. Her face was a frozen mask, nostrils flared, lips parted. Her eyes widened until they were enormous—in mute appeal and naked terror they looked to Chance.

He went white. Raw agony twitched over his face and darkened his eyes. His hand fell to his side, clenching into an impotent fist. With a thud he dropped the gun.

For the first time in his life, Eden knew that Chance Mallory had admitted defeat.

CHAPTER
TEN

A STOREY and a half beneath Julius Paxton's house of delight, all was silence—and flame. The dank cellar was lit solely by twin torches leaping high from ornate brass bowls. Beside them was a gong, a tongue of golden fire curling across its surface.

On either side of the heavy door stood a row of young Chinese men. Save for the glistening black braids, their heads were shaven, their bodies encased in black silk tunics and trousers. They were one with the silence and the flame, so still as to be carved of stone, the hatchets they held giving back the fire's reflection again and again. None of them moved as the door swung wide to admit Julius Paxton's ward.

Eden was surrounded by the almond-eyed maidens, flanked fore and aft by guards garbed as were the others, their faces as impassive. With their hatchets, they motioned her to the dungeon's only chair, a tufted ottoman hung with silk.

The women bound her ankles, tied her hands behind her. Eden watched them with desperate eyes. But no spark of feeling touched the empty masks of their faces.

Only one, as she passed again through the heavy door, looked quickly past Eden and into the room itself, sudden, stark terror in her eyes. Then the girl fled—and with a creeping horror, Eden gazed about her.

Her heart constricted. Back to the wall, his wrists

chained above his head in heavy iron fetters, was Chance.

Across the flames, his steely eyes held hers—and in his gaze was all the rough tenderness of his remembered caresses. Eden's lips parted and shaped his name—but it was a shape without substance, for the name was not uttered.

'And how do you like my special chamber, my dear Eden?'

Softly Julius entered the cellar, the weight of terrible things in his words. As the precise syllables echoed into the gloom, a pulse began beating visibly in the hollow of Eden's throat.

'This room has many interesting functions. Chief among them, the punishment of any unruly slaves. You'd be amazed at how persuasive a lash or two of the whip on a soft back can be—or a touch of hot iron to delicate flesh.'

Julius crossed to Chance. Once again he removed his spectacles and for a long moment the two men looked into each other's eyes—Chance's stare so cool, so contemptuous, the careful features of Julius Paxton twitching and jumping. With shaking hands he replaced his eyeglasses.

'You have quite a reputation as a fighter, Mr Mallory,' Julius said, his words grating like a knife being pulled slowly from its sheath. 'Let's see how well you do against one of my men! If you win, you save my ward's life. But if you lose—she spends tonight at my mercy and joins you tomorrow in a watery grave.'

Julius whirled and clapped his hands three times in succession. At this signal, one of the guards stepped forward and unchained the prisoner.

Slowly Chance bent his arms at the elbow, clenching and unclenching his fists. A grim smile stretched tight across his lips.

Almost Eden could feel his renewed vigour flowing through her own veins—feel his determination. He was ready for what lay ahead. Ready for battle. No more would he have to war with the whispering shadow of evil that was Julius Paxton. It was a flesh and blood man he would face now.

Again Julius clapped his hands in three successive bursts and now one of his men hastened to sound the gong.

The door swung open. From the shadows beyond, ever soundless, emerged Chang. He bowed to Julius, then slowly he drew back the flowing sleeve from his left arm.

Eden started. In a kind of paralysis of terror, she stared at Chang. Where a hand should have been glittered a hook. Razor sharp, it glinted wickedly in the torchlight.

In frozen dread Eden realised how carefully Julius Paxton had spun his web of evil—how carefully he had wound even this last thread about them.

'Please—' she murmured, but she could go no further —and her desperate silence was a kind of wordless, formless prayer.

As if he were a cat readying himself to pounce, Chance took position in a springing half-crouch. Like two pin pricks the reflected fire gleamed in the depths of his eyes. Still as a stone statue, the Oriental faced him, the flames dancing over his implacable face.

Silently the two men stood, motionless. Then, slowly, warily, his eyes shining like jet, Chang began to stalk Chance. For the space of several seconds, the two circled each other, glances locked. Eden's own eyes darted from one to the other, her throat constricted, her heart pounding out painful beats.

'*Aaaaaiiiieeee!*'

From stillness to breath-stopping action, Chang sprang, his cry—the first sound Eden had ever heard him utter—rending the air, curdling her flesh.

Lightning-swift, Chance fell back, but the Oriental came again. Chang whirled here, there—he was everywhere, his hook seeming to menace Chance from a dozen different directions at once, slicing through the air like a snake's venomous tongue.

Chance dodged him, feinting right, left, his body always a fraction away from danger. His movements were controlled yet fierce, his mouth set in a rigid line.

Played against the flickering torchlight, the flashing figures cast monstrous, leaping shadows on the dungeon walls. The mens' harsh breathing, the crackling of the flames—only these sounds broke the silence.

Eden strained forward, her whole body tense with silent supplication. The wrench of the rope burned her skin, but the pain was a negligible thing. Only Chance mattered. And always that same whispered prayer rose from her lips. 'Please—'

Hook aloft, Chang charged. Too late Chance turned —the hook found his shoulder and pierced it, drawing a quick spurt of blood.

Eden heard his hard onrush of breath. Like a gaping wound she felt his pain in her own body.

Staggering slightly, Chance fell back against the wall. Then he clenched his teeth and pushed upright. Once more Eden saw the Oriental charge.

'*Aaaaaiiiieeeee!*'

But swiftly Chance dodged aside and this time the hook grazed only air. Chance whirled, striking Chang a powerful blow across the shoulders. The Oriental plunged to his knees. He fell. Motionless he lay against the ground.

Chest heaving, Chance wrenched a hatchet from one of the guards. In two swift strokes, he sliced through Eden's bonds. Then, unable to stay upright a moment longer, he fell to his knees before her. With an inarticulate cry, Eden cradled his head in her lap, her tears falling against him.

'How touching,' Julius said viciously. 'But he needs to be on his feet for the next opponent.'

'No!'

Eden sprang up, shielding Chance's body with her own. 'You can't make him fight again—not after all he's been through tonight!'

One hand on the ottoman, Chance hauled himself up. He was swaying where he stood, yet still he roused the strength to grind out savage words.

'Bring on your next man, Paxton.'

'Foolish pride!' Julius spat out scornfully. 'It was always that way with you. I remember—'

Sharply, Julius caught himself up. He nodded to one of the guards.

'Wah Lee, rechain the prisoner. Perhaps the next contest would be more amusing if Mr Mallory is rested, his wounds tended to.'

'And the girl, master?'

Julius' thin eyebrows arched into sardonic crescents. 'Let's leave them alone, shall we? To enjoy their last minutes.'

Julius spun on his heel, his men moving in a silent

column behind him, the last lifting the inert body of Chang. Face down, the Oriental bounced against the black, silken back, the sleeves of his tunic falling long over his menacing secret once more.

The door shut heavily. In the flame-filled stillness, Eden looked to Chance and what she saw wrenched at her heart. The welt on his cheek had opened anew, his shirt was ripped to the waist, his gashed shoulder running red.

Swiftly Eden was across the room. With a kind of tender anguish, she smoothed the sweaty tangle of auburn hair from his forehead and her voice held heartbreak.

'What have they done to you—'

A brief smile moved between the stubble of burnished beard and moustache. 'You're safe and Paxton hasn't broken me—nothing else matters.'

The door opened, and Eden saw a girl leave a bowl of water and linen strips on a tray and withdraw again. Lightly Eden ran to fetch the tray. She lifted the bowl, holding the water high before Chance. He drank thirstily, then set back his head and shut his eyes.

Eden bent. Dipping one of the linen cloths in the water, she wrung it out and with careful strokes bathed the blood from his face and shoulder. She took up a clean bandage and staunched the wound, then bound it.

'I failed you, Eden,' Chance said, and his voice was soft and hoarse. 'I let him trap me—take you—'

'No! No!' She shook her head, the black hair shifting about her shoulders. 'It's I who am guilty! You're here because of me.'

Chance turned his head aside. 'You're wrong. The score Paxton is settling with me tonight is an old one.' He paused and a muscle clenched hard in his heavy jaw. 'Julius Paxton is my half-brother.'

Eden stared at him. Wildly her thoughts beat back to the fierce hatred she'd first felt pulse between the two men that night on Nob Hill—and then again in the cellar of that dismal brothel. Truly it was as thick as blood . . .

'Julius' mother was a Nob Hill aristocrat. My mother was only a Barbary Coast saloon girl—but it seemed Cornelius Paxton couldn't keep his hands off her!' Chance laughed on a harsh note. 'She never told me who my father was—she never told me anything. Not until she got sick. One night when she was feverish— delirious—I learned everything. Paxton wouldn't let her alone. He lied to her, told her he loved her, but when she told him she was expecting a child— Well, that was the last time she ever saw him.'

Chance stopped and swallowed. Wincing, Eden saw the pain from old, remembered wounds stark on his face, and as he opened his eyes she saw, too, the naked torment in his gaze. With a special agony of her own, she waited for him to go on.

'I—I went to Paxton Place to beg—food, money —anything to help her.' His voice fell to bitterness. 'My father gave me a job in the stables.'

He began to twist his hands against the iron fetters, the pain in his eyes replaced now by a hot wild glow, as if he, too, were burning up with fever. The fever of his past.

'Somehow Julius found out who I was. He made my life hell! He baited me—tormented me—gave me every filthy job he could think of. When I tried to fight him the only way I knew how—with my fists—he ran. He ran like the coward he is! But first he set two of the older servants on me. I took my first beating at Paxton Place that day, but it wasn't the last. And the worst of it was, day in, day out I saw the luxury they lived in—I saw their greed! While all the while my mother was wasting away in a Barbary Coast rathole!'

His voice was growing in violence with every word he spoke, with rage in his face and eyes blazing fiercer, stronger. They were no longer alone for the dungeon now was filled with angry ghosts, spectres from a past that had not been laid to rest. That perhaps would never be laid to rest.

'I never forgot those days at Paxton Place. Not the beatings or the insults or the way they lived—sitting like gods in their Nob Hill mansion. While down on the Barbary Coast—'

He broke off and his silence held a bitterness, a suffering, mere words couldn't contain. When he continued, his voice scraped like flint on stone.

'I remembered everything. Everything! Each time I got into the ring I saw their faces in front of me—the father who'd left my mother to rot, the brother I hated. Each time I got into the ring it was as if I was fighting them—fighting back! Fighting for the pride they'd denied me!'

'Hush!'

Eden laid soothing fingers against his lips. Once more she pressed a cool cloth to his burning face. 'You must save your strength.'

He looked at her, his eyes boring into her very soul.

'I saw you for the first time when I was working at Paxton Place—you came in a carriage with your parents. You couldn't have been more than seven or eight. You were dressed all in silk . . . I stared at you and you looked right past me— as if I was so far beneath you I wasn't even there.'

The same hatred that had pricked Eden's memory the night of the banquet showed again in Chance's gaze, a hard, simmering hatred Eden knew now had built up within him day by day, year by year. A hatred she knew she had first seen as a small girl that day in her parents' carriage.

She had forgotten the time, the place, even the boy, but that hatred—so driving, so intense—that she had remembered all these years.

Chance's voice turned savage.

'I never forgot that girl. Eden Cortland became Nob Hill to me—with her silks and satins and her high and mighty airs. I never forgot the girl or the way she looked at me. Like I was an animal.'

His eyes narrowed, his voice taking on a low, throbbing chord.

'And then I heard you were coming back to San Francisco. The night I broke into the party, I told myself I was doing it to rile my brother, but I knew it was to get a look at you! And when I saw you there—dressed in silk and diamonds, like some beautiful statue—it was like the first time all over again. I wanted to humiliate you —the same way you'd humiliated me. I wanted to break you! That's why I dragged you off to the Golden Gate.'

Chance drew in a rasping breath. 'God, how I despised you!'

Before that smouldering rage, Eden did not flinch and the eyes that rested on his face were tender.

'And do you despise me now?' she asked softly, steadily, searching his face, her own longing laid bare before him.

Sudden, searing desire beat across his hawklike features.

'I only wish that I did.'

Trembling, Eden reached up her hands to his face —the face she had caressed again and again in her dreams. Slowly she traced slender fingertips along his creased brow, the grooves at his eyes, the tight lines of his mouth, the seamed cheeks.

'I remembered your touch,' Chance said and his voice was husky with suppressed emotion. 'I remembered everything after you'd gone—the feel of your body —the way your hair fell about your shoulders. The rose scent of your skin—'

In wonder Eden looked at him—and in the darkness of that chamber, in the finality of those moments, all that had been as a barrier between them fell away. In the urgency of the present, the past crumbled. There could be no pretence now, for now was all they had.

Flinging away all that had gone before—of her past and his—Eden came to him. 'I remembered, too,' she whispered, 'everything.' Gently she laid her head against his chest—and this time he did not hold himself away.

Whatever was to come, whatever lay ahead, they would have these moments. Moments stolen from the vice of death, moments sought and claimed without thought to the future. Moments dark with the shadow of separation. But moments that were yet theirs alone.

Eden lifted her head and, her eyes holding his, she pressed her hands against his back, caressing him with a voluptuous slowness.

'Don't Eden,' he rasped, 'don't add to my torment—'

But there was longing in his eyes and face, a longing stronger than his words. He bent his head, his mouth crushing hers hungrily, his lips and body holding a rough urgency.

With a matching desire—with a need born of despair —Eden wound her arms around his neck, pressing close to him with desperate abandon. A convulsive shudder shook through Chance's body, and hers too, and together they strained against time and place to claim those moments left to them.

And then they heard the door swing open.

Eden's arms tightened, the transient joy fled from her face. But there was an answering strength in Chance's eyes—a fleeting tenderness.

'Don't worry. I won't let them have you.'

But it was not her fate that frightened Eden but his, and she clung to him—until two of Julius' men dragged her, struggling away.

Fiendishly smiling, Julius looked at her. 'Perhaps before the next battle begins, we should give the gentlemen a taste of what they're fighting for.'

He shot out a swift hand—and in one deliberate thrust, tore Eden's kimono from neck to hem.

In a small, instinctive gesture of helplessness, Eden's hands lifted and opened. Near numb with shock, she stared at the scarlet folds that lay like a red pool about her feet. Then sharply she dropped to her knees, clutching up the silken remnants to her body. On her face was the bruised look of stark shame, and around her neck, like a cruel jest, Julius Paxton's diamond pendant still hung intact.

With an inarticulate roar, Chance lunged forward —remembering too late his manacled wrists. Gasping, he fell back to hang there helplessly, chest rising and falling in rage.

Julius laughed. With a leisurely stride he stepped close to Chance. Brother looked at brother. Down all the days of their lives they faced one another. For the last time, they took each other's measure.

Each encounter, every angry meeting had led them surely and relentlessly, step by inevitable step, to this moment. And in that moment the silence between them seemed to stretch to all eternity. In that moment time hung poised.

Then, still with that leisured demeanour, Julius lifted a hand. He paused, hand held high, and, smiling, struck Chance hard across the face.

'That, dear brother,' he said softly, 'was something I've long wanted to do.'

A corner of Chance's mouth shot up with cool insolence. 'I see you waited until I was chained up to try it.' He gave a short laugh, saying with a wealth of insolence, 'You're still a damned coward.'

The blood drained from Julius' Paxton's face. A muscle twitched once in his cheek. 'And you're still Barbary Coast scum!'

Julius stepped back. He nodded towards Chance, motioning to one of the guards with a convulsive jerk of his hand. 'Free Mr Mallory and let's get on with things. I find I'm growing weary of this whole matter.'

The guard obeyed, then three times again Julius clapped his hands. The gong was sounded. The door swung wide. But on the threshold stood not one of Julius Paxton's minions—but his mother.

'Your game is over, my son,' Lenore's voice was a ringing bell. 'Yes—your game is surely over!'

Julius did not reply, merely stared at her with the first tinge of fear Eden had ever seen him reveal.

With resolute steps, Lenore came forward, looking neither to the right nor the left, but only towards her son.

And, as she came, a profound silence fell over the chamber.

They were all a part of that silence. Chance, standing riveted. Eden, still kneeling, still clutching the scarlet stuff of her kimono to her body with one hand. The black-garbed guards. All of them frozen like figures in a tableau. All of them watching Lenore.

Her unbound grey hair streamed over her shoulders, her dress was a strange, floating thing, tattered and ragged and stained with dirt. Her drawn face was ashen, but her eyes were gleaming—biting clearly into the murky darkness about her.

In one frail hand glittered a gun, while a torch was held high in the other. Like some avenging angel of flame, she stopped before Julius.

'You have bought and sold your last slave, Julius —you have committed your last act of evil. Your reign is ended—your kingdom is about to crumble about you.'

Julius' lips drew into a bloodless line that cracked into ravaged halves the sculpted oval of his face.

'By whose hand, Mother?' he asked with a scorn that was almost bravado. 'An ill, mad old woman?'

Lenore shook her head.

'No, Julius, I'm neither sick nor crazed—though you and Chang almost drugged me into believing I was both! You gave me my first injection of opium on the day of your father's funeral—a sedative to calm my nerves, you said! Daily you increased the amount until my mind was so clouded I could no longer think. But gradually I saw through your scheme. I persuaded Chang to let me administer my own medicine—and then I only pretended to take it. How I suffered those weeks! But my mind is free now.'

She came close, staring into Julius' glittering face.

'I escaped my prison once before, remember? And stole away to Eden's room. Quite by accident I ruined all your careful planning that night. Well, I've escaped again—and for the last time! I crawled out of a window and followed you here and now—when you're so close to victory—I'm going to snatch it from you.'

Lenore halted, pausing to take a shuddering breath. Though her face was tight with pain, she went on with a terrible determination.

'You see, I know all about you, my son, all about your hate and anger—your warped and twisted soul! I've always known, from the very beginning. I lied to myself at first . . . I tried to pretend it wasn't true. But finally I had to face it—I had to accept what you really are—' She faltered, but only momentarily.

'Yes, I've always known—that's why you drugged me, wasn't it? To keep me silent. I know how you bought up all the property you could on the Barbary Coast—as if in that way you could destroy your brother—his world. I know you owned the building that housed Chance Mallory and his mother. And I know you started the fire that killed her.'

Eden's breath strangled in her throat, sick horror churned her stomach. She heard a groan escape Chance's lips that was almost a sob. His powerful hands were clenched hard at his sides, as if to hold himself rigid against his hate. There was death in his eyes.

'I know you plotted to kill your father,' Lenore went on softly. 'Poison, wasn't it? Deftly administered by Chang. You killed him to become Eden's guardian—to carry out your plan of revenge against Chance Mallory.'

'Yes,' Julius answered her, his features contorted, his

small, slim hands writhing together. 'I killed my father —I loathed him! All his life he preferred his Barbary Coast bastard to me. I can still remember the day he told me who Chance Mallory really was. "I wish to God Chance was my rightful heir," he said. "You'll never be half the man your brother is!" '

A small sound caught deep in Julius' throat, but whether it was the sound of anger or strange, macabre laughter they could not tell.

'I'd see him standing at the window, watching Chance, and I'd hear his words, over and over, pounding in my brain, "You'll never be half the man your brother is!" I can still hear those words . . . They haunt me day and night—they never let me rest . . .'

There was a whispered fury in Julius' voice that made Eden's flesh crawl. A fury that had driven Julius Paxton down a hundred pathways of revenge. His voice rose, the hard, taut sound seeming to scream into the dungeon.

'Yes,' Julius said again, 'I killed him!'

Abruptly the startled silence was broken by the thud of running feet. The heavy, soot-smudged figure of Seamus Muldoon bolted through the door, a company of armed men, equally grimy, behind him. Over their shoulders peered Julius Paxton's slave girls, their delicate faces bearing the stunned look of those awakened too suddenly from a nightmare.

'Boss!' Seamus tossed Chance a gun. 'We gotta get outta here—the whole upstairs is burnin' like pitch!'

As though to emphasise his words, thick smoke began to drift through the door and into the chamber.

'I set the fire!' Lenore cried triumphantly. 'I freed Mr Mallory's men! Your evilness will end forever tonight, my son!'

'Will it?' Julius demanded. 'Will it indeed?'

Three times in violent succession Julius clapped his hands—and at the signal, the guards leapt to action. As one, the white men swarmed to meet them.

'Will it indeed,' Julius murmured again, his voice strangely soft.

With the coiled swiftness of a snake, Julius Paxton sprang forward and wrenched the gun from his mother's hand. Caught off balance, Lenore stumbled. The torch dropped from her grasp—falling against Julius.

His small body sparked to flame. His head pitched backwards his arms thrashing heavenward. His agonised screech cut above the crack of gunfire and screaming still, his back a mass of flame, Julius fled through the door.

Lenore crumpled. 'My son,' she murmured brokenly, 'my son—'

Darting towards Lenore, Eden caught the woman as she fell, half dragging her, half carrying her to where the band of slave girls stood huddled. Lenore sobbed out anguished, distraught words.

'I loved him—in spite of everything, I loved him. In spite of everything he was still my son—'

Comfortingly, Eden drew Lenore's head to her shoulder, the other women clustering around them like frightened children. The earthen chamber was filled with smoke, the clashing guards and white men moving through the acrid air like ghosts in a hazy dream. Tensely Eden searched through the murk to follow Chance's swift figure.

Though outnumbered, leaderless, Julius' men pressed on doggedly until, driven to the wall, those still standing threw down their weapons and fled into the holocaust above.

Gasping, his face half-hidden in the dense light, Chance found Eden. In one hand he held the clothes of a fallen guard. Swiftly he thrust them at her.

'Put these on.' His voice was harsh with urgency. 'And hurry. Our only way out is through the maze that runs underneath all of Chinatown—this cellar is a part of it. I used the tunnels myself when I was doing a bit of smuggling.'

Eden nodded her understanding. Without ceremony, she let the kimono fall and dragged on the tunic and trousers.

Chance seized her hand and pulled her into the passageway, Seamus following with the featherlight form of Lenore Paxton in his arms. Behind them surged the caravan of white men and Oriental women.

With one hand Chance felt along the walls, searching out a path. His other hand stayed firm about Eden's own, and to this she clung.

Chance's shirt was soaked with sweat and streaked with soot, but his pace never slackened. With grim resolution he led them along the smoke-clogged labyrinth. They inched through tunnels, around corners, down stairs. And all the time the smoke grew denser, hotter.

It became harder to breathe, and harder yet, their every breath was full of searing fumes that burnt the lungs and throat and sent tears streaming from reddened eyes.

Chance halted, calling a command over his shoulder.

'On your knees! The good air is near the ground!'

They fell to the floor, crawling on all fours to claim the reserves of smoke-free air.

Eden felt her limbs like leaden weights, felt the heat like a never-ending inferno against her skin. Every pore was on fire. Her hair was plastered to the nape of her neck, her tongue thickening in her throat. Ahead lay only smoke and blackness, more heat, more weariness. Her head was swimming with fatigue, she longed to drop where she was. She couldn't drag her body another foot . . . she couldn't.

Yet, eyes on Chance, she did.

Then, just ahead, they saw a small thread of light, barely flickering through a slatted window. Lifting an arm to muffle his face, Chance hurtled up the stairs and kicked through the bamboo slats. Fresh air cut thinly through the smoke.

Chance turned and reached down for Eden, lifting her in his arms and swinging her through the window. In utter exhuastion, she dropped to her knees, breathing in great, deep lungfuls of sweet, clean air.

One by one the others emerged from the tunnel. As the last one reached safety, Julius Paxton's house of evil fell into a pile of burning rubble.

That April morning came in many different ways to the city of San Francisco.

On the edge of Chinatown it was heralded by the pealing of the tower bells of Old St Mary's Church. Over the hills to the East, it swept in with long, pink ribbons that dappled the sky and dissolved the night. Across the bay it came like a golden embrace.

In the produce district morning erupted with the babble of a dozen different dialects, Chinese, French, Russian, Italian, Armenian. Along the residential streets of the middle class, it was rung in with alarm clocks and trolley bells. Inside the summit-crowning mansions of the wealthy, morning crept quietly into the kitchens and servants' rooms—and left the master's quarters alone.

But on the rowdy streets of the Barbary Coast that April morning—as all mornings—came unnoticed.

It was a few minutes after dawn when the slatted doors of the Golden Gate saloon swung suddenly wide, admitting a strange company of begrimed men, dazed Oriental women, and one Nob Hill lady in the black tunic and trousers of a Chinese warrior.

'Honey!'

Butterfly Sloan's jubilant voice preceded her across the floor. She shoved through the room, pushing against the crowd to throw her arms around Eden in a crushing hug.

'Honey, I been on pins and needles ever since Seamus and the boys took off. You look like something the cat dragged in—but you're alive and safe and that's all that matters!'

Butterfly swung around to face Seamus Muldoon.

'You hardheaded old goat!' she smacked a resounding kiss on his flat forehead. 'You did it!'

Seamus ducked his head and as the others laughed aloud, he blushed in pure pleasure.

'Missy Boss! You fool gel!'

Black braid bouncing in vehement underscoring to his scolding, Ah Wan scurried up to Eden. 'Fool gel! Running away—no say where you go! No sense! Running away from Golden Gate—fool gel!'

Eden smiled at the shrivelled little man, then, remembering that this was not how the game was played, she compressed her face into firmness.

'Ah Wan,' she began briskly, 'you will please look

after my guests.' Eden ushered Lenore and the other women forward. 'See that they're made comfortable. They need something to eat and somewhere to sleep —and some clean clothes.'

Ah Wan threw up his hands in utter defeat.

'More gel bosses!'

Butterfly linked her arm with Eden's, then triumphantly she led the smoke-stained company through the gilded room.

'Free drinks for everyone!' the redhead bellowed, pounding a fist on the bar. 'We're celebrating! And the first swallow better be for the Boss.'

Butterfly shoved a bottle down the polished length of the mahogany bar and grinned up at Chance, pride and affection glistening on her painted face. 'You look like you could use a stiff one.'

'I could at that,' Chance agreed dryly. He accepted the bottle, poured out a glass and drained it. Then slowly he set it down and his glance sought Eden's.

Hot blood darkened her cheeks, her breasts rising and falling as she struggled for breath. She turned away. Her mind was filled to the brim with memories of the long night—the touch of his arms and how she had sought them, the words they had spoken.

Yet what if that touch and those words were but a part of this night of terror, and nothing more. What if that touch and those words held no more substance than the curling clouds of smoke that had filled Julius Paxton's dungeon.

What if all they had shared proved as fleeting as the night wind . . . the night mist. What if, like a dream, all that had passed between them should vanish with the first light of morning.

What if she should awaken from that dream to find Chance Mallory unchanged—and uncaring.

Slowly Eden lifted her head, and in the shimmering glass behind the bar she saw Chance. There was the same springing keenness to his powerful body as there had been before the fight with Chang, a glint to his eyes—sharp, alert. As if he, too, were waiting—hoping —for some sign, some word, he stood watching her.

Eden felt swift need rise up within her. But balanced on a precipice between that need and her pride, she hesitated.

Abruptly Chance swung his eyes away from her. Eden followed his gaze upward, to where the chandelier had begun a strange swaying. A sharp splintering sound jerked her attention back to the mirror and she saw that a jagged crack had cut it in two, shattering—separating —their reflections.

Choking fear consumed her. She cried out—but her words were throttled by the ominous rumble beginning to rise above the mad noise of the Golden Gate. Louder and louder the sound grew, until it held all the terror of a train rushing at full speed. Until it rolled over them all in roaring waves.

The walls were trembling, the floor was shifting, shuddering. A thin, long-drawn out wail of horror vibrated through the shivering room.

'Earthquake!'

Eden saw Chance's strong hands extended towards her. Desperately she reached out to him. There was no hesitation now—but now was too late, for even as they touched she felt the world slip away from beneath her feet and she was flung across the room.

CHAPTER
ELEVEN

Now the chandeliers were swinging like pendulums, the furniture careening crazily, smashing to and fro. As if the waves of the ocean billowed beneath it, the floor was undulating—rocking—buckling.

The room was pitching, people lurching, stumbling, crying out in mindless fear and panic as they reeled helplessly.

Eden was thrown to the floor. She heard Chance shout her name and frantically she answered him, rising to her knees and stretching out her arms to him across a sea of shattering glass and falling plaster. And then her cries strangled in her throat as she saw him fall beneath a shower of crumbling masonry.

Over and over she screamed his name, but her scream was only one among many, all of them swallowed in the deafening roar of a disintegrating world. She struggled to her feet, trying to fight a path across the swaying room—trying to fight her way to Chance through the avalanche of smashing brick, splintering wood.

Almost she had reached him when the ominous sound of creaking timber sheared the air. Slowly the ceiling beams began bulging—bending—sagging downward.

'Miss Eden!'

Seamus grabbed her about the waist. 'You've got to get out of here!'

Furiously Eden twisted against him. 'Let me go! Let

me go! Don't you understand? I've got to help Chance!'

But Seamus said nothing, merely catching her in his arms and carrying her to the street. Fighting like a mad thing, Eden wrestled out of his grasp to take two frantic steps towards the Golden Gate.

But even as she ran the ceiling began to shift and split. As if they were no more than matchsticks, the fluted columns snapped in two, crumbling to dust. Back and forth, in and out, like a living thing, the gilded palace swayed.

Eden halted, her body quivering like a drawn bow —and her anguished sobs were drowned in the slow rolling thunder of the collapsing walls.

Her knees buckled. Turning as she fell, Eden crumpled against Seamus' burly chest. Beyond tears, she stood trembling silently against him.

Awkwardly Seamus patted her hair.

'Maybe he's all right, Miss Eden—maybe he got out and we just didn't see him.'

Eden looked up and into Seamus' face, that flat, ugly, fine face brimming now with the need to believe his own words.

'Perhaps he did,' she said softly. 'Perhaps he did.'

She turned away from him, sweeping the street with eyes burning black as coals. A violent shudder shook her body.

What had been was no more. What was left was the landscape of hell. The pavements were buckled and broken, the streets gashed and cracked open.

Buildings had twisted on their foundations, roofs and walls tilting crazily, chimneys toppled. Like an emptied eggshell a brick structure stood, its façade sheared off. As Eden watched, it slowly crumbled inward, smashing the wooden shacks beside it—burying a flood of victims beneath it.

Sickened—dazed—Eden swung away. Around her the survivors roamed the wreckage like hollow-eyed ghosts, half-clad, dishevelled, screaming, sobbing out names, calling to those who could no longer hear— questioning those who were beyond caring.

'The end of the world! It's the end of the world!'

'Help me! Somebody—please help me!'

'Mother! Mother!'

'My child—have you seen my child?'

'Have you seen my wife?'

'Have you seen my husband?'

'Have you seen—'

Some knelt by the crumbling ruins, praying for the dead already buried—frantically hunting for those who might still be alive.

From within the heap of rubble that had been the Golden Gate, Eden saw a sudden, small movement. She swayed—Seamus quickly grabbed her arm.

With a single, sharp thrust, she threw him off and ran forward. Plunging to her knees, Eden clawed at the twisted pile of bricks and wood until her hands were bruised and bleeding. Until her fingers touched a man's still face.

She reeled backwards as the dead eyes, open and staring, met her own. One hand came up to her mouth.

It wasn't Chance. This time it wasn't Chance. But perhaps somewhere, at this very moment—

The earth, still for some minutes, began to shake again. A crescendo of screams met the aftershock, a grinding roar rent the air. Bricks, once loosened, began a precarious swaying, buildings swinging to and fro like trees in a gale—shattering, collapsing. Above the wreckage, columns of smoke began drifting skyward.

Fire—fed by clapboard tinder and sawdust floors, fuelled by the quake's debris, escaping gas, the tangle of fallen wires—was beginning to rage through the Barbary Coast. And beyond.

Seamus lifted Eden to her feet. Urgently, gently, he said, 'You've got to get away from here, Miss Eden—to where it's safe. People are headin' for Golden Gate Park—it's clear there.'

Without blinking, Eden stared at him.

'I won't leave until I find Chance.'

Seamus smiled patiently. 'I'll stay and look for the Boss. You didn't think I'd leave him, did you?' His arm came about her waist. Like he might a stubborn child, he prodded her forward. 'You go with Miss Butterfly and Ah Wan. They'll take care of you.'

Eden took a few stumbling steps. She halted. Just beyond Butterfly's beckoning hand she saw Lenore Paxton's frail form crushed beneath a fallen beam.

But Eden could feel no sorrow. It was only an empty shell that lay there—the woman's soul had died long before. And perhaps in death she would find the peace that had for so long eluded her in life.

Lenore Paxton. Only one among so many the quake had claimed. And was Chance Mallory another?

No!

The word screamed through Eden's mind, her body staggering from the violence of the protest.

If Chance were dead I would know it, she thought fiercely. The tie that bound us binds us still. If he were dead, my own heart would stop beating.

Consumed with feverish energy, the terrible, frantic

need to do something—anything—Eden plunged reck-
lessly into the throng of refugees jamming the streets.
Wordlessly Butterfly and Ah Wan followed her.

Coolie and mandarin, dock worker and saloon girl
and matron—they came, all fleeing the earthquake's
destruction, the fire's threat. All seeking safety.

But would anywhere in the world ever be safe again?
The earth had been swallowed whole by a swaying
monster—spewed out as a gnarled and broken thing,
spitting forth flames.

The homeless, the stunned, the grieving, they all
trudged the same twisting road, all clutching the few
possessions they had managed to snatch from the
quake's path.

A woman in best bonnet and nightdress toiled along
beneath a bundle of pots and pans and bits of crockery, a
Bible atop it all. An old man in a red union suit hauled a
steamer trunk behind him. A child cradled the family
dog in skinny arms, a dude in an opera cape swung a
violin case in one hand, a basket of food in the other.

The sound of their footsteps was a constant drumbeat
against the cobblestones, the groans of the wounded, the
keening of the bereaved, the mindless mutterings of the
shocked and stunned rising like a single roar from their
ranks.

Always there were more joining the line, each one
bringing bits of news.

The quake had broken the water main. The hoses
were dry. The fire was devouring the Barbary Coast,
Chinatown, the Mission District, the waterfront. San
Francisco was under martial law, General Funston,
commander of the Presidio—the city's military preserve
—had been placed in charge. His men were comman-

deering all carriages and automobiles to haul water from
the bay, to carry the wounded. They were using dynamite to try and stop the blaze.

In the black tide of surging humanity, Butterfly's
green satin dress was a splash of gaudy colour—of life,
her red head was held high.

Eden's face was set, her body and heart constricted by
an iron band. But her face was fierce with hope. As she
walked she whispered the same words over and over, as
if they were some magic incantation.

'He can't be dead . . . if he were dead I would know
it.'

And, as onward they all plodded, the columns of
smoke multiplied above them, the crackling of the
flames sounded ever louder about them, the sky glared
always brighter above them.

The exodus ended in the green grass of Golden Gate
Park, the refugees sprawling exhausted on the ground.
Here the soldiers were already beginning relief oper-
ations. Here Eden found an outlet for the restless fever
that possessed her.

There were blankets to be distributed, children to be
comforted and cared for. There were food lines to
mobilise—cauldrons of coffee to brew, bread to bake,
stew to stir.

The wounded were stretched out on crude litters, and
for long hours Eden walked beside a nursing sister, basin
and towelling in hand. All through the night, as Butterfly
slept in the open air, Ah Wan curled at her feet like a cat,
Eden stood within a small, stifling canvas tent that
housed the operating table. A swinging lantern provided
the only light. Chloroform was the only anaesthetic.
Water was scarce—medical supplies even scarcer.

There was little to do but bandage and pray.

And with every prayer Eden uttered—those to ease the dying from life, those to comfort the pain of the living—went a plea for Chance Mallory.

Every time she turned over a man's strangled body, she knew an instant of paralysing fear. But it was never Chance. Every time she ladled out a plate of stew or a mug of coffee, she looked up in anticipation. But it was never Chance.

Dawn came, the blazing sun as brilliant as the flame-tinted sky and sea. Dawn came and with it a stream of fire fighters poured into the park. Half-dead from exhaustion, yet they stopped only long enough to wolf down a plate of food.

Dawn came and with it more refugees, more news.

They were pumping water from the bay through a series of interconnecting hoses. The Palace Hotel was gone. Market Street had been lost. Nob Hill was going.

'The whole dang city is burning,' a bleary-eyed man muttered as he took a serving of stew from Eden's hands. 'The whole dang city . . .'

'San Francisco is licked this time for sure,' his companion assented and down the line voices rose in morose agreement.

With a thump Butterfly set down her kettle of coffee.

'Licked are we?' she demanded angrily. The redhead swung around to the front of the line. Hands on her hips, she glared at every soot-streaked refugee, confronting them all.

'So things are burning up, huh? Tumbling down around our ears, huh? Well, so what! We've been down before—and we came out of it okay. And we'll come out of this, too—you just wait and see! And when we do, we're gonna build a brand new city—bigger and better than the old one! We're gonna build the best damn city in the whole United States!'

'You tell 'em, Miss Butterfly!'

Surging forward, Seamus gave the redhead a vigorous nod of approval, his three-tiered nose quivering in righteous agreement. 'You tell 'em all!'

With a joyful cry, Butterfly threw off her apron and ran to Seamus. In wild delight, she gave his massive shoulders a whack. 'You big lummox! You're a sight for sore eyes.' She wiped a hand across her gritty forehead and grinned. 'Whew! What I wouldn't give for a cigar.'

'Seamus—'

Spoken through stiffened lips, Eden's single word was less than a question, more than a plea. Slowly she came towards him, her eyes growing larger and darker as she waited for his words.

Before that burning gaze the man's face creased in pity—his own eyes wet with the tears of a personal agony. He shook his big head, croaking out a broken apology.

'I'm sorry, Miss Eden. I—I couldn't find any trace of the Boss.'

Dawn had come . . . but with it came no news of Chance Mallory.

Abruptly Eden whirled. With flying steps she was across the park—and the pounding of her feet and the thudding of her heart beat to the same desperate rhythm.

He must be alive—he must be—

'Honey!'

At the familiar voice, Eden halted. Head erect, shoulders braced, she turned. There was a flush of high colour in her cheeks, a sudden, bright snapping glitter in her eyes. At the resolve shining on her face, Butterfly nodded.

But the redhead said nothing. With the clear, hard-headed vision of a woman wise in the ways of the world, she understood everything—she always had. And now, without asking, she knew where Eden must go. What she must do.

Butterfly gripped Eden's shoulders, her fingers biting deep with encouragement. 'Good luck, honey,' she whispered.

CHAPTER TWELVE

EDEN plunged into the holocaust.

Beneath a lurid sky she walked, down streets thick with cinders and ash and flaming wreckage, every minute marked by the deafening roar of dynamite ripping through reddened clouds.

The blasts shook the earth beneath her feet, sending torrents of sparks exploding skyward to drift down around her shoulders. The smoke seared her nostrils, the heat scorched her skin. This was hell and she was in it, but she pushed on, through the crowds of dirty, bedraggled, desperate humanity.

And of every aimlessly wandering refugee, she asked the same question.

'Chance Mallory, the Barbary Coast fighter—have you seen him?'

And always came the answer. 'Sorry, Miss, can't say that I have.'

Of every khaki-clad solider, shepherding the crowd, maintaining the fire line, she asked the same question.

'Chance Mallory, the Barbary Coast fighter—have you seen him?'

And always came the answer. 'Sorry, Miss, can't say that I have.'

She searched the emergency hospital tents set up on every corner—straining her eyes over the faces of every man lying there, living and dead. And of every nurse, every doctor, every minister that roamed the ranks of the wounded, every priest, she asked the same question.

'Chance Mallory, the Barbary Coast fighter—have you seen him?'

And always came the answer. 'Sorry, Miss, can't say that I have.'

She staggered through the rubble of a hundred buildings, she stumbled over the tangled heaps of maimed and broken bodies, looking into hideously burnt faces with frozen resolve. And of every man clearing away the debris, hauling out the dead, she asked the same question.

'Chance Mallory, the Barbary Coast fighter—have you seen him?'

And again and again and again came the answer.

'Sorry, Miss, can't say that I have.'

Sorry, Miss. Sorry, Miss. Sorry—

Night came, the fire's glare deepening to a tawny glow, the tall flames casting wild, leaping shadows that chased each other across the twisted world. Night came and still Eden searched and walked and questioned.

Her back was breaking, her legs buckling, the voices of the crowd—the thunder of dynamite—the crackling of the fire rising and falling in indistinguishable waves around her, the smoke-thickened air shimmering before her in dancing waves.

Still she walked and searched and questioned until she could go on no longer. Slumping against the charred ruins of a wall, she looked with red-rimmed eyes up and down the streets that had once teemed with roaring life. There had stood the Silver Dollar. There the Paradise. There the Red Rooster. There . . . the Golden Gate.

As clear as a bell Eden heard Ah Wan's voice floating

over the wreckage of the Barbary Coast.

'Bad things coming for this city! I go Chinatown—see it in the cards—bad things coming!'

He had been right. The end of the world had come.

She dropped her head in her hands and from beneath closed eyelids her tears fell through interlaced fingers. 'Chance—' she whispered—and she knew then the truth she'd been afraid to face.

He must be dead . . . and she too numb to know it.

'My dear child! You shouldn't be out now—it's far too dangerous! I'm afraid looters and thieves are roaming at will.'

Eden struggled to open her eyes. Surely this must all be a nightmare, this smoke-filled world, these formless, blackened ruins . . . And the man before her—was he, too, a part of her nightmare?

'I'm Father Chandler. I run the mission here.' The small, spindly priest—a man in miniature—reached for her hand. 'Come, child—'

Quickly Eden pulled away from him, her strangled voice near hysterical with weariness. 'I have to keep on! I—I have to find someone—'

Father Chandler smiled into her protests and his touch on her arm was soothing. Gently he began leading her away from the rubble and down a flight of rickety stairs. It was cool and dim within the cellar, the moans of the wounded echoing faintly through the gloom.

'You can rest here tonight and have something to eat.' He steered her towards an empty bed. 'And then in the morning you can begin searching again.'

Eden shook her head, struggling through her exhaustion to make him understand. 'I—I can't rest until I find him, Father, I—'

Suddenly she stopped. The colour drained from her lips, her hand coming up in an oddly abrupt motion to clutch at the base of her throat.

At the end of the corridor was a small alcove, and in the alcove a single bed. On the bed was Chance Mallory.

Eden's heart leapt—and checked. Through a confusion of joy and fear she looked at the Priest. 'Father —he isn't—'

'No, no, my dear,' Father Chandler assured her swiftly. 'Mr Mallory is quite well. He's only catching some much needed rest.' He chuckled ruefully. 'I'm afraid he tried to save the Barbary Coast singlehanded.'

'Father,' Eden whispered urgently, 'would it be all right if I stayed with him? I won't disturb him, I only —only—'

The stooped little man smiled.

'I know.' He patted her hand. 'Your search has come to an end, hasn't it?'

Eden nodded, such happiness welling within her heart she thought she could not bear the joy of it. Knowingly the priest turned away and as he went, Eden skimmed quickly down the corridor. By the side of the bed she paused.

Chance lay with one leg bent, an arm flung over his head. His long body was twitching convulsively, his face, shadowed by several days of growth of beard, was taut and strained, as if even at rest he waged some inward battle of his own making.

Eden sank down beside him.

This man had hurt her, degraded her, sent her to the depths of a humiliation she'd never known before— raised her to an ecstasy she'd never believed possible. He'd condemned her to death and with one touch had brought her back to life. And from it all one thing had emerged as a true, ringing certainty.

Here, in this odd, nether world of shadows, surrounded by strangers, Eden Cortland had come face to face with the reality of her heart.

All she wanted from life was to share it with Chance Mallory. On whatever terms he offered her.

Tentatively she reached out a hand. Now there was no tremor from the depths of the earth, no madman's scheme of revenge to keep her from Chance. Gently her hand came against his face, and as if to soothe away his tortured restlessness, she stroked his cheek.

'Rest easy, my darling,' she whispered, and as on the night of the fight, he seemed to reach across a void of time and space to hear her.

Chance sighed deeply, his own hand reached out to cover hers—and then he was still.

Pillowing her own head on the bed beside him, Eden slept.

He was gone when Eden awoke. She pressed her palms to the empty bed, its contours still bearing the imprint of Chance Mallory's body. Then swiftly she stood and ran down the corridor, calling out in hectic fear.

'Father Chandler!'

On creaking knees, the priest arose from a woman's bedside. He was nervously fingering his black rosary beads, his knobby face harried with worry. But his voice still held a soothing calm.

'Your Mr Mallory is out fighting the fire again, my dear.' He shook his head. 'It's spread even closer—I'm afraid we'll have to evacuate soon.'

Eden raced past the priest and up the stairs, his last

words ringing unheeded behind her.

'Be careful—it's an inferno out there!'

The world was a red haze, a restless wind blowing in from the bay to whip the virulent flames to a frenzy, skyrocketing them a hundred feet in the air.

It was a pitifully small force that fought the blaze. With grim determination they drove their hoses into the fire—where they had no hoses, they beat at it with gunny sacks and horse blankets, blistering their hands as they worked.

On Chance Mallory's flame-lit face, Eden read impotent rage—burning fury. He was fighting for the Barbary Coast—fighting to save his world. But these enemies could not be defeated by animal strength or street cunning.

Unchecked the fire rampaged, aided and abetted by the treacherous sea breeze that sent it leaping from one wooden building to the next—that spread the pall of smoke and cinders like a deadly virus.

The fire roared forward, sparks igniting the frame structures on either side. Snakes of flame curled high against the sky, arching over the mens' heads, repelling them.

Muttering a ferocious oath, Chance fell back—and with a muffled cry, Eden surged against him.

A moment only would she hold him and no more —but for that moment she must feel his hard body close against hers. She must know he was safe and whole.

But his arms did not come about her.

Quickly Eden looked up and into those eyes that for so long had eluded her. No longer did they blaze with hatred . . . now there was nothing in their depths.

With the carelessness of a stranger, Chance Mallory

looked down at her. Within the circle of her arms, his body held only indifference.

'You're putting on quite a show,' he said with casual mockery, 'What would your high-tone friends out East say?'

'Chance—' Eden said and could say no more. Though her lips were parted to speak, she could not seem to grasp the words.

Looking at her coldly, Chance reached up to the arms still twined about his neck. Deliberately he unclasped them, and his low, heavy voice had a flinty preciseness to every syllable.

'Just what the hell did you come here for anyway?'

As if struck, Eden fell sharply back. The confusion on her face shifted to pain, and in the eyes that searched his face for some trace of what had been, her heart was plain.

'I—I came to find you,' she faltered. 'The last time I saw you—'

'The last time you saw me,' Chance finished for her, 'I was buried beneath three feet of rubble. Well, I appreciate your concern, but as you can see, I survived.' A gleam of self-mockery lit his eyes. 'I seem to have more lives than a cat.'

He swung slightly away, forearming the sweat and soot from his face. 'And now that you've found out that I'm all right, you can be on your way, Miss Cortland.'

'You called me Eden two nights ago,' she said, her low voice like a brand of flame from the raging fire—the words torn from her soul.

'Did I?' He shrugged. 'Well, my advice to you is to forget that night—forget it ever happened.'

'No—' Eden murmured wildly, shaking her head

against his casual words.

There was a raw, bleeding wound where her heart had been—an aching hollow at the very core of her. The world was falling into fragments about her . . . desperately she tried to gather up the pieces.

'No!' she cried again. 'No, I won't forget it—I can't! I can't forget the way it was with us—I can't forget that you risked your life to save me—'

'I did what I did to ruin my brother's plans,' Chance cut in ruthlessly, 'not to save your skin.'

He looked back at her, and against the crimson glow of the sky, his rough-hewn face was blank—wiped free of all feeling. With studied cruelty, he went on.

'Get this straight, Miss Cortland, nothing happened between us that night—nothing that matters. When you're staring death in the face, you reach out to any woman that's handy—you don't care if she's a lady or a Barbary Coast whore.' He laughed on a harsh, careless note. 'Like I told you before, in the dark, one woman's just like any other.'

Eden stifled a cry. Her slender body was swaying, as if from the impact of his words. The reddened world around her seemed to recede into small specks of waving colours and distant noise . . . then slowly it came back.

Beneath the black brows, Eden's eyes glittered with an unnatural brilliance. One hand came up hard across her breast, rigidly she turned.

'I see,' she said stiffly, 'I see.'

Painful understanding was dawning.

In those last seconds before the quake, she'd wondered if all that she and Chance had shared in the depths of Julius Paxton's dungeon would vanish with the morning light. Now she knew the truth.

She'd been ready to give herself utterly to this man
—spirit, soul, body and mind. She'd been ready to place
before him all that she was. Only to find at the very
moment of her surrender that he didn't care to claim the
victory. She was to him what a hundred other women
had been and would be. And no more.

She'd felt bound to this man by a tie that not even
death could dissolve. But now she knew that bond was
but a gossamer web, woven from the threads of her own
longing—her naïveté.

Last night *had* been a dream—a mist-filled fool's
dream that reached back to that first moment she'd seen
Chance Mallory framed against the fog. And his tenderness—their shared caresses—those had been but a part
of the dream.

This brutal stranger—these brittle moments beneath
this blood red sky—they were the true reality. They
always had been.

Well, he must never, never know how completely
she'd been his. He must never, never suspect that she'd
been ready to throw her pride at his feet—for now that
pride was all she had. Like a precious raiment, Eden
gathered it to her.

Her head swept up, her hands falling to studied
gracefulness at her sides. It was the old Eden who
answered him—regal, controlled, her voice and bearing
eloquent of her manner.

'I wouldn't feel too highly complimented, Mr Mallory. Yes, I came to you—in the darkness of a dungeon
—in desperation! And that's the only way I'd ever dirty
my hands with a Barbary Coast ruffian. You see, in spite
of what you think, there is a difference between a lady
and a slut!'

Eden turned again to look at him and the cold scorn in her eyes was like a slap across the face. 'But of course you couldn't be expected to know that—raised as you were, fighting like an animal in the ring for your liveli-hood.'

From around her neck, Eden tore the diamond neck-lace Julius Paxton had hung there so long ago. Carelessly she dropped it on the ground at his feet, and her words—summoned up from the welter of her pain and humiliation—were a lethal blow.

'This should cover your troubles for the other night. I'm sure you're not above grovelling in the dirt for payment—considering that's where you've spent most of your life.'

Chance Mallory's tough, hard body tightened—there was the kindled fire of cold steel in his blue eyes, his lips were bitten together in a thin line. Tall and straight he stood before her, cold, silent, with nothing flickering across his falcon's face.

This, Eden knew, was how he must look to an oppo-nent facing him in the ring.

Then in two violent strides he was at her side, looming over her, and as he seized her shoulders, his hands shook with suppressed violence.

'I could take a horsewhip to you for that,' he said, his voice dangerously soft.

A sudden explosion rent the air. Chance's eyes blazed with the reflected fury of the showering sparks. For an instant Eden thought he would strike her—almost she wanted him to. She wanted to feel hatred for him surging through her veins.

She wanted to hate him as much as she loved him.

Eden threw back her head, rousing her pride to fight

down that love—and her clear, ringing words were the mark of her triumph.

'I would expect no more from a former stableboy.'

A muscle clenched taut in Chance's jaw—his hands went rigid. For the space of several heartbeats he stood motionless, and Eden could hear his heavy breathing.

Abruptly he broke away, dropping to one knee to lift the jewel she'd thrown down before him from the scorched earth. With a gesture so brutal she winced, he grasped her hand and thrust the diamond into it.

'Keep your damn Nob Hill trinket,' he said savagely, 'it will pay for your trip back East.'

Eden drew a sharp, audible breath.

'Back East,' she repeated disbelievingly, forcing the words through stiffened lips. 'You think I'm returning East?'

'Why not? The Golden Gate is gone. Paxton is dead.' His eyes narrowed. 'There's nothing for you here.'

Silently Eden looked at him.

With every fibre of her being she was willing him to give her one word—one look—to show her that in spite of his words, he harboured some small spark of feeling for her. Even now—had he met her one fraction—she would have given herself to him. Gladly.

But he gave her nothing.

Her white face wearing a mask of aloof dignity, Eden nodded at him—the kind of cool, curt nod ladies use to their inferiors—and her ice-water words were ones Harriet Phelbert would have been proud of.

'Goodbye, Mr Mallory—I trust we won't be meeting again.'

Eden turned on her heel and started away. The diamond was still clutched in her hand, its hard edges cutting into her flesh, and she welcomed the pain—using it as a goad to keep her head erect, her shoulders squared, to keep that light, uncaring tread she'd once known so well.

She could not look back—not even for a moment. One final glimpse and she would be vanquished, defenceless before him. She must keep on.

But half blinded by hot tears, she stumbled. Her control shattering, she began to run, through blood-coloured clouds of smoke, through a pandemonium of noise and flame, and before her wavering gaze was the image she would hold in her heart for all time—the memory of the man who would own her forever.

The memory of the savage, careless stranger who didn't want her.

She thought she heard Chance calling her name over and over, but she knew it was just her own inner longing that she heard—the voice of her pain. Her desire.

She thought she heard footsteps behind her, grinding hard, and she increased her pace to a frenzy to escape them. No one must see her tears—her humiliation.

On she ran, through a spray of cinders and swirling black smoke, until heartbreak and weariness swept over her and she fell against the charred wall she'd sought as a refuge the night before.

She doubled over, choking—fighting for breath—struggling against her sobs. One after another the blasts of dynamite ripped the air, Eden's body jerking convulsively at every roar.

Tongues of flame licked her skin. Crackling heat beat down on her. She jerked up her head and the dazzle of a hundred suns glared in her eyes.

She was ringed by fire—fire that writhed closer every

second. And through the shimmering heat she saw a man and the man was Chance.

No. No! He was a vision only, born of her desperation, created by the churning smoke, the dancing, dizzying flames—her own need.

Desperately Eden flattened her body against the wall —and so swift was the crumbling of the bricks above her, so sudden, she had time for only one frozen look upward before they crashed down around her.

CHAPTER
THIRTEEN

AT FIRST it was Father Chandler Eden saw bending above her. But his tiny frame misted and blurred and became a pair of deft hands that prodded her, poked her, his kindly voice turned into the authoritative tones of a nursing sister.

'She's suffered some bad bruises . . . She needs rest —cold compresses . . .'

The sister dissolved into darkness. Once again it was Father Chandler who was there. But he was murmuring words Eden could not seem to grasp. Bit by wavering bit his face was fading into a black haze. She tried to clutch him back—hold on to him—raising halfway from the bed.

Then a blazing heat—a white hot light—engulfed her. She was chained to a stake, ringed by a circle of fire. Madly she struggled, screaming—until her spirit soared above the flames and she was riding in a carriage.

She was seated between a man and a woman. Eagerly Eden turned to first one and then the other. But they were faceless—no more than stuffed mannequins. Eden screamed—but her scream was no more than a whisper.

Yet at the sound, the boy who was holding the plumed horses turned. He was not faceless—a hatred was burning in his eyes as fierce as the flames that threatened her. But Eden did not care.

He was something strong and real and she reached out her arms to him—but once again the fire embraced her, threatening to suck her back to the stake.

She writhed away, escaping to a schoolroom lined with books and dotted with desks. At every desk was a girl in a middy blouse and a blue serge skirt, a black bow in her hair.

The Academy? Yes—yes! Surely here, Eden thought, she would find refuge. But as one after another of the students turned to her, Eden saw they were faceless —insubstantial—dissolving to dust at her touch.

She ran down the aisles—and into a beautiful room filled with shimmering women and sleek men. But these men and women didn't speak. They didn't move. Above the satin *décolletage* and black broadcloth coats, they, too, were faceless—formless—

Only one man held any reality.

He was framed by the fog, wind stirring about his strong figure. There was hatred in his eyes, but strength in his hands—and Eden knew that here was someone who would fight for her.

He was coming towards her. He was battling through the fire that ringed her. He was calling her name and at the sound of his voice, Eden was no longer afraid.

He lifted her in his arms and carried her from the fire and into the cool dimness of the mission—and then darkness and the hot demons overtook her once more.

Again . . . and again Eden would hear a voice calling to her through the flames—that strong voice she had heard before. She would cling to that voice as she had clung to the man, and as if by the power of that voice, she would be lifted from pain and the terrible heat to a cool plain.

Then into her dimmed consciousness came buzzing voices.

'We'll take care of her now, Mr Mallory—you really must have a doctor attend to those hands, to wait any longer would be to risk infection. I promise you, Mr Mallory, she'll be all right—'

Remembrance hit Eden like a blow.

It was Chance Mallory she had seen in the flames. Chance who had called her name. Chance Mallory with his savage face and careless words.

Chance Mallory, who must never, never know how much she loved him . . .

She sprang up at him, beating at him, screaming at him to go—to leave her. Screaming that she hated him—screaming a thousand incoherent things. And through her screams she heard the voices again.

'You really must leave, Mr Mallory—you're only upsetting her. We'll call you if she asks for you.'

And then he was gone—and now Eden knew she must struggle unaided to free herself from the pillar of fire. Now she must battle back her pain alone. But she was too tired—too tired . . . Need swallowed pride and she cried out for that remembered strength.

'Please! Please, I want—I want—'

'Yes, child?' Father Chandler answered her. 'What is it you want?'

But swift remembrance came to Eden's aid. She wanted Chance but he didn't want her—and no one must ever know it.

'There's no one, Father,' she whispered, 'no one . . .'

Once again the hot pincers began tearing at her, biting at her. Once again the fire came licking through the shadowed depths of her mind to claim her.

Then suddenly that pain-misted, flame-filled mind was rent by fire whistles and bells.

'No! No!'

Eden came to screaming consciousness. She sat bolt upright, pressing her hands to her ears—but nothing could drown out the wild shrieking.

She swung her legs to the edge of the cot, dizzy from the sudden exertion, but as she would have pushed to her feet, Father Chandler was at her side.

'Father!' Desperately Eden gripped his hands, but this time he did not fade into darkness. 'Father, we must evacuate! The whistles—the bells—don't you hear them? They're so close! We must evacuate—'

Still holding her hands, the priest sat on the edge of the bed. Above the roaring noise, his voice was vibrant. 'They're sounding that signal all over the city, child! It means the end of the fire!' His grip tightened about hers with fervent triumph. 'Do you understand? The fire's over—we've won! The mission—the whole of San Francisco—is saved!'

Eden fell back against the bed. Her hands dropped. Framed by the tumbled hair, her face was without belief, her shadowed eyes dazed. When finally the victorious shrieking dimmed and died out, she questioned the priest in a voice as weak as a mewling kitten's.

'I—I don't understand. How can the fire be out—'

'You've been here for two days,' the priest interrupted her gently. He laid a hand against her forehead, then nodded approvingly. 'Your fever's broken at last —you'll be mending more quickly now.'

Two days . . . for two days she'd been in the grip of a fever.

Eden passed the back of a hand over her forehead. Slowly recollection was returning—the terrible sound of the falling bricks, the crushing weight against her flesh—

The man fighting towards her through the flames.

No—no. Chance Mallory had been but a part of her delirium, and nothing more. She would be a fool to think anything else—and she was done with foolishness. Rent by sudden inner torment, Eden thrashed restlessly against the pillow—and as she did, her eyes caught a winking gleam on the bedside table.

The priest followed her gaze to the diamond pendant. 'You were holding that when you were brought in.'

Like black magnets, Eden's eyes held the jewel. She stretched out a shaking hand and gathered up the gem, clutching it to her, and into her mind came the memory of words as crystal hard as the diamond itself.

'Keep your damn Nob Hill trinket. It will pay for your trip back East.'

Abruptly Eden held out the pendant.

'Father, there is something you can do for me.' Her voice was low and swift and clear. 'Sell this.'

Somehow it seemed only proper that her guardian's legacy should provide the means to return Eden Cortland to Philadelphia.

Eden sat in a wooden tub, soapy water to her waist. How wonderful it felt finally to soak the earthquake's grit from her skin! Gingerly she ran the soap down her arms, her breasts, but in the week since she'd been at the mission, her bruises had faded to a murky yellow, her flesh no longer tender to the touch.

Yet as a result of her illness, she seemed to hold a new fragility, her features finely drawn, the thick, shining mass of her freshly washed hair appearing to burden her small head. As she stepped from the tub, her naked body gleamed like a piece of delicately carved porcelain. But inside was only icy resolve.

This was the day Eden Cortland would take up her old life.

Clad in a borrowed cotton dress, Eden left the mission without a word to Father Chandler—and that was according to design. The coldness within left her no room for words.

Her next step in the carefully prepared plan was to seek out the fashionable dress salon of Miss Wilhelmina Frazier—now no more than a patched-together shed of scorched sheet iron and cardboard.

Miss Wilhelmina, an owl-eyed mistress, had made a fortune sewing exclusively for a Nob Hill clientele. With supplies rescued from the quake, she was already on her way to making a second fortune catering to those same women—now left literally with nothing but the clothes on their backs. On the spot—and for a hefty price—she made up a travelling ensemble for Eden.

Clad in Miss Wilhelmina's mauve silk creation, Eden looked approvingly at her reflection in the hand-held mirror. Yes—she would do. Eden Cortland would return to Miss Phelbert's as elegantly turned out as she had come.

Yet there was a difference.

She had arrived in San Francisco wearing her stylish aloofness like a mantle—now that façade had become a mirror of her inner emptiness.

She had begun changing the morning she'd awakened from the fever to the mad ringing of fire bells. Daily her shell had hardened—until she was no longer flesh and blood, but a graceful automaton, well-bred and elegant. And utterly without life.

Eden Cortland had become the perfect graduate of Miss Phelbert's Academy—and it had taken a Barbary

Coast fighter to complete her education.

With a gait as correct as her garb, Eden left the dressmaker's and embarked on the third and final part of her plan. Carefully she picked her way down the rubble strewn streets of what had once been the Barbary Coast.

All around her dozens of hands were busy cleaning away the debris. Dozens more were busy rebuilding, slapping fresh paint on charred bricks, setting up businesses in tents and tar paper shacks.

There was still no electricity, no gas, no running water, but the Barbary Coast had joined the rest of San Francisco in turning its eyes away from the blackened ruins. Away from death and towards life—the streets that only days before had rung with the sounds of destruction, now hummed with the noise of hammer and saw and hope.

'All bets in, gents! Keep your eye on the card—every corner squared!'

Blithely straddling a wooden crate, Butterfly Sloan sat in the centre of a blanket-hung tent. A cigar was poised at the corner of her rouged lips, and from the faro box that rested on the barrel-supported plank before her, she was snapping out cards with practised deftness.

'And jack wins! The winner is jack!'

As disappointed murmurs rose up from the crowd, Butterfly looked briefly up from her cards—to see a small, elegant figure coming slowly towards her. She beamed a smile, waving the betters away with a flick of her cigar. 'Game's over, gents! Shoo!'

Quickly the redhead broke away to Eden.

'Honey! I wondered when you'd show up—why, I ain't heard a word from ya since you sent that note to the park almost a week ago! I wrote you back that the boys and I had come down here and set up shop—why didn't you look us up sooner?'

Without waiting for an answer, Butterfly tossed her head towards the crude tent. 'What do you think of the joint? Ah Wan, Seamus and I are partners—can you beat that? I deal faro, Ah Wan reads the fortune cards and Seamus—well—' She snorted out a laugh. 'The big lummox just kind of looks after us all.'

Butterfly took Eden's gloved hand in a warm grasp.

'How about it, honey? Can we cut you in for a share? We'd sure love to have you—'

Quickly Eden fell back. 'No, thank you—I have no interest in being a partner again in any kind of Barbary Coast establishment.'

At the sharp gesture, at the brief, cool words, Butterfly's painted eyebrows shot up. She gave Eden a long, slow, head-to-toe look. Pointedly she went on.

'You were dressed like that the first time I saw you, honey, all prim and prissy. But I could tell right off you were an honest player—there was something good and clean in your face, something living in your eyes. But now—'

She broke off and turned on her heel. Settling herself on the crate, she began again to rifle through the cards, slicing out hard words. 'So what did you come here for anyway? It sure ain't a social call.'

'I came on business,' Eden said formally. 'I recently disposed of a—personal item—and since in a sense Mr Mallory and I are still partners, I thought it only fair that he receive half the profits.'

Eden reached into her reticule and withdrew a stack of bound bills, placing them neatly on the plank before Butterfly. 'I tried to send a message to Mr Mallory, but no one seems to know where he can be reached. I'm leaving for the East tonight, and I thought perhaps you would see to it that he gets the money.'

Butterfly looked briefly at the bills, then turned once more to her cards, shuffling and reshuffling. 'You don't think the Boss'll touch a penny of that dough, do ya?'

Eden snapped her reticule shut with a pronounced gesture and her voice was crisp.

'I no longer care what Mr Mallory does or does not do. My obligation to him ends with the payment of this money.'

Butterfly sprang to her feet, the cards spraying into the air around her. 'So you don't give a damn about Chance Mallory, huh? Well, I don't believe it—any more than I believe the way you're acting!' She gripped Eden's shoulders. 'I know why you're leaving, honey—I know what the Boss said to you! But can't you understand? The quake took everything he had—he don't have a plug nickel to offer you!'

Butterfly began shaking her, as if by the power of her hands she could force a spark into those empty eyes, force life into that brittle body—as if by her fierce words she could somehow break through that hard shell.

'I think it's high time you found out something, honey! I know dang well where the Boss is—we all do—but he made us swear not to say a word to you! He's been at the emergency hospital the army's got set up at the Presidio all week—Seamus is fetching him back right now.'

For just an instant, Eden's heart lurched to life. Urgent questions throbbed against her throat. Then into the tense moment broke the raucous strains of the *Mississippi Rag*.

A roar went up from the street, people surged towards

the ragged band of musicians—their song seeming to embody the wild spirit of the town that had once been. And would be again.

Sharp as a knife, the music cut at Eden, bringing with it the torment of a thousand memories—and that remembered pain strengthened her resolve. Her face settled again into that cool, closed mask, and her voice was the voice of one bred to a polite uninterest in her inferiors.

'How unfortunate. But as I said, Chance Mallory is no longer any concern of mine.'

With a sound of profound disgust, Butterfly threw up her hands and spun around. She shook her head, tossing words over her shoulder as scalding as acid.

'Suit yourself, honey, but just remember—pride won't warm your bed on a cold winter's night.'

Eden fell back sharply, her hands coming up to clutch at her breast. The spectre of a memory was rising before her. She had heard those words somewhere before.

It had been a cultured voice that had spoken them —smooth and well-bred, but a desperate voice—a voice lacking life.

Eden turned. She began walking—without aim, without direction—almost without knowledge, her feet moving as if of their own volition. Her chest was tight, her head pounding those words like an iron band about her body.

'Pride won't warm your bed on a cold winter's night.'

A heavy fog was rolling in from the bay, curling around her ankles, swirling to her waist, her shoulders. swallowing the streets one by one, its grey tendrils carrying a damp chill. The sodden clamminess ran up Eden's spine, but she did not feel it.

The air was wet and still, heavy as a shroud, but Eden

moved through it blindly. As if from far away, voices sounded, lights flickered, but they did not pierce her consciousness. Darkness was falling, and if she had wandered for days or hours she did not know—she did not care.

She was alone in the world, chasing the ghost of a memory that floated always before her—that trembled on the edge of her consciousness.

'Pride won't warm your bed on a cold winter's night.'

Then suddenly through the grey mist came the dulled sound of foghorns. Quite clearly the scent of the sea was borne to her nostrils.

She halted, her heart pounding so hard against her corset stays, she thought they would burst.

She had felt that mist—she had smelled that scent a hundred times in her dream. But now her dream had become reality and with that reality was born a re-membrance as illuminating as a bolt of lightning—so violent it ripped away the veil that had hung forever before her eyes.

Now she knew who had spoken those words. It had been Tyler Cortland—her father. Now she could look clearly down all the years to see him sitting straight and slim beside the small Eden.

He had taken her for a carriage ride—the first time he'd ever taken her anywhere. The first—and only —time he'd ever sought her company.

He'd dismissed the liveryman and driven the rig him-self, not through the fashionable section of Nob Hill, but through streets she'd never been to before. Streets that glittered and sang and jumped, pulsing to the rhythm of jangling banjos and scraping fiddles.

Round-eyed Eden had stared at the garish gambling

palaces and painted women. She was not afraid—a feverish excitement was whirling within her. And on her father's face, that usually stiff, handsome face, she saw for once an eagerness that matched her own.

What a wonderful, wonderful night! She was alone with her father—and he was smiling and happy.

'The Golden Gate,' he'd said, pulling up before the noisiest, the gaudiest of all the noisy, gaudy buildings. 'It's half mine—and it will be half yours someday. But you must never, never tell your mother—you must never even tell her that I brought you here. Promise?'

Solemnly the young Eden had promised.

Then her father had driven on, towards the bay, and as he went he began to speak to her of strange, sad things.

Things, she realised now, he'd had to tell her for he had no one else—things he'd bottled up all his life and, save for this one night, he would carry to his grave.

'I haven't been a good father to you, Eden, and I know it—but I haven't anything to give you—there's nothing inside of me to give! I live in an empty world, Eden, filled with empty people! Oh, they look splendid enough, but take away their fine manners and pretty clothes and there's nothing there—nothing to hang on to! And I'm as empty as the rest of them . . .'

He'd pulled rein and turned his head towards the water, the mist curling about them both like a cloak, the sea air heavy in their nostrils.

'I have a certain standing in this community, Eden, a certain respect. I have a house that's a palace and a wife who's the envy of every man I meet.' He'd laughed on a note so bitter she'd shivered. 'If only people knew! My place in society is a sham—it's built on lies! There's no more warmth in my wife than a winter wind—my house is as empty as a tomb! If only I had the courage to give it all up . . .'

One hand had come up to his forehead and in his whispered words Eden heard a vast sadness.

'Only down here—on the Barbary Coast—can I be happy! Happy in a way I never will be on Nob Hill! Oh, I can't come here often and I have to be discreet, but when I am here I feel reborn! The people here are real—they love, and hate. They feel!'

Tyler had clutched Eden's small hands, and though his eyes were blazing, his grip was as cold as the night air, his flesh as chill as a dead man's.

'That's why I'm leaving the Golden Gate to you, Eden—so that some day you'll have everything I threw away—everything I sacrificed on the altar of pride! Remember, my daughter, always remember—pride won't warm your bed on a cold winter's night!'

Eden began to walk again, quickening her steps to keep pace with her frantic mind.

All her life she'd tried to escape the image of that night—locking her mind so tightly against it, against that bitter man and his desperate words, that she'd allowed no part of the past to penetrate. Allowed herself no memories at all.

But the essence of her father's words—that terrible longing—that she'd never been able to forget. It had haunted her through the years. It haunted her still. Like darting, clutching ghosts those words echoed in her heart.

Empty people. Empty house. Empty world . . .

How well she understood her father's world! It had been the world in which she'd been raised—the world to which she was returning. For a few white-hot moments she'd found her way free of that world—but now there would be no escape, no way out.

As bleak as her father's voice—as grey as the dripping mist—Eden saw her life stretch out before her.

She would teach at Miss Phelbert's. She would marry. And everyone she met—everyone she knew—all her life—would be filled with people as brittle and empty as those sawdust mannequins that had peopled her delirium. As brittle and empty as Eden Cortland herself.

A gust of wind stirred suddenly through the shrouding fog, lifting it. Rising up like the map of her future, Eden saw the ferry building in the distance. She drew a deep, shuddering breath and started forward.

And then she stopped.

Just ahead, half turned from her, was the figure of a man. A tall, strong man, with heavy arms and broad shoulders and a jutting profile that seemed to challenge the mist.

It was Chance Mallory—and at the sight of him Eden drew up as still as a stone. It wasn't fair! It wasn't fair that she must see him now—just when she was so close to winning free. Why couldn't he have allowed her to leave in peace—why must he prolong her torture to the very last?

She had thought the heart was gone from her body—she'd thought she'd been granted the wish made on the night she'd left the Golden Gate—no longer to feel.

But now she knew she'd been lying to herself. For the feelings she had thought gone forever were flooding her body with a searing agony. The heart she had thought dead was twisting in savage pain.

In that moment she wanted Chance Mallory more

than she had ever wanted him before.

Her only salvation lay in going quickly—quietly—
before he turned and saw her. She took a step backward
—yet her hungry eyes clung to him, memorising the
planes of his face, the set of his body—storing up
memories in the secret places of her soul.

Just as she was about to turn, her eyes fell on his
hands. They were swathed in bandages to the wrists.

Eden's eyes widened as she stared at those hands—as
she remembered Butterfly's words. 'He's been at the
emergency hospital the army's set up at the Presidio for a
week—'

But how had he been injured? Hope battled against
despair as she struggled to fit together the pieces. Had it
been—had it been as he pulled her from the burning
rubble of a crumbling ruin?

Her bosom began heaving wildly. She clutched a hand
to her heart. Her silken toque had long since been
claimed by the night, her hair was spilling to her shoulders. Her skirts were damp to the knees, the fashionable
suit torn and stained. In a mad disarray of mind and
body, Eden came towards him.

'Chance—'

At the sound of her voice his body jerked convulsively. She heard him draw a sharp breath.

'What are you doing here? I was told you were leaving
tonight—I thought you were on the ferry that just pulled
out.'

Eden came close to him—so close she could see the
rigid outline of his jaw. 'I'm not leaving until you tell me
something,' she began with laboured breath. 'I want to
know—I must know! That day at the mission—was it
you who pulled me from the fire?'

For an endless time he did not answer, and as she stood there—waiting—Eden felt the world around her holding its breath.

Then into the fog Chance's voice fell thickly, the words so low they scarcely reached her.

'Yes—I was the one.'

A soundless sob caught deep in Eden's throat. Slowly light was breaking. He had told her he didn't want her—then risked his life to save her, disregarded his own pain to give her his strength.

Over and over Chance Mallory had done one thing and said another, but he was a man who spoke not through words but actions, and in those burned hands was the vivid proof of what he had sacrificed for her.

She looked again at those hands. Hard, calloused hands that had carried her from the emptiness of a Nob Hill mansion and to the truth—that had brought her out of a Barbary Coast jail and to safety.

Bloodstained hands that had battled in the ring to right her mistake—that had battled for her life in a dungeon. Smoke-stained hands that had led from her an inferno and to freedom.

Hands that had fought through hellfire for her.

His back and shoulders were tensely set—stiff with the same pride Eden knew only too well, a pride that had made her order him from her bedside—kept her from calling his name when she needed him so desperately. A pride that had almost sent her from him forever and into a life of barren emptiness.

But Eden Cortland would not sacrifice her love on the altar of meaningless pride, for from his grave her father had given her the gift—the blessing—he'd denied her in life.

She reached up a shaking hand to Chance's rock-hard back.

'Butterfly told me why you said what you did—why you sent me away. It's because—because you feel you have nothing to offer me isn't it?'

Chance swung violently around, shaking off her touch, and his rugged face was hollowed, creased with torment—the face of a man on the rack. 'Yes—yes, that's right.'

He jerked his gaze from her, biting off his words through set teeth.

'I love you, Eden—I've loved you from that moment I saw you sitting next to Paxton—glittering like a diamond, hard and beautiful—and out of my reach! I loved you—and I wanted to hate you!'

Chance drew a harsh breath.

'I tried every way I knew to force you out of my mind. Those weeks after the fight, I wandered around the waterfront—drinking—brawling—But I wanted you so desperately I had to come back. I wanted you—but I couldn't tell you. I had to punish you—I had to punish myself! After you left the Golden Gate I used to stand outside Paxton Place just trying to get a glimpse of you—I came here tonight just to get a last look at you. When I saw the ferry pull out I thought I'd lost everything—'

'You haven't lost me,' Eden said softly. 'I'm not leaving you—not tonight—not ever.'

With a convulsive gesture Chance brought up his bandaged hands. Through the masking heaviness of his voice, Eden could hear the throbbing undercurrent —and she knew what it cost him to speak.

'You've got to know—the doctors say I may never

fight again. I haven't even got my skill in the ring to offer you.'

Tears hung glistening in Eden's eyes, all of her being gathered in that black gaze. With a gentle urgency she whispered, 'I thought maybe—maybe you were done fighting. Fighting the past—fighting your feelings. Fighting me.'

Slowly Chance turned his head to look at her. His back to the fog, the auburn hair blowing about his rigid profile, he looked as he had on that first night—hard, unyielding.

Then into that burning gaze came the dawning of a new peace.

'Perhaps I am,' he said quietly and there was wonder in his voice. 'Perhaps I am.'

Awkwardly his arms came about her. Wordlessly Eden laid her head against his chest. Once more—and forever—she felt her stirring desire answered by his need. Once more she felt that pulsing current beat up between them—a bond of love so strong it had won through the flames of the past to bring them to the oneness of this moment.

Through the thinning mist the ravaged outline of San Francisco rose stark around them—but from the ashes of the old city a new one would rise. And they would be a part of it.

'I can't give you what you deserve, Eden,' Chance began unsteadily. 'But know this—from that first moment you've had my whole heart. You always will.'

Eden lifted her head, her hands coming gently against his face.

'That's all I'll ever want,' she answered him simply— and there was no need for any more words between them.